# WAYSIDE SCHOOL
## BENEATH THE CLOUD OF DOOM

# ALSO BY LOUIS SACHAR

*The Wayside School Series*
Sideways Stories from Wayside School
Wayside School Is Falling Down
Wayside School Gets a Little Stranger

Holes
There's a Boy in the Girls' Bathroom
Fuzzy Mud

*The Marvin Redpost Series*
Marvin Redpost: Kidnapped at Birth?
Marvin Redpost: Why Pick on Me?
Marvin Redpost: Is He a Girl?
Marvin Redpost: Alone in His Teacher's House
Marvin Redpost: Class President
Marvin Redpost: A Flying Birthday Cake?
Marvin Redpost: Super Fast, Out of Control
Marvin Redpost: A Magic Crystal?

# WAYSIDE SCHOOL
## BENEATH THE CLOUD OF DOOM

# LOUIS SACHAR
## ILLUSTRATED BY TIM HEITZ

HARPER
An Imprint of HarperCollinsPublishers

Library of Congress Control Number: 2019026618
ISBN 978-0-06-296538-7 (hardcover)—978-0-06-296540-0 (lib. bdg.)—
978-0-06-299523-0 (special ed.)—978-0-06-299977-1 (intl. ed.)

Typography by Catherine San Juan
20 21 22 23 24  PC/LSCH  10 9 8 7 6 5 4 3 2 1
❖
First Edition

*For Ruth*

# TABLE OF CONTENTS

# A NOTE FROM THE AUTHOR

This is the fourth book about Wayside School. I wrote the first one, *Sideways Stories from Wayside School*, more than forty years ago.

I'm a lot older now, but in my heart I'm still Louis, the yard teacher, passing out the balls and playing with the kids at recess.

To fully enjoy this book, you should read the other three first, wait forty years, and then read this one.

Or you can just read it now.

# 1

## THE BELLS OF WAYSIDE

It is very important that the children at Wayside School know the bell system.

The first bell in the morning sounds like this: *WHOOP-WHOOP! WHOOP-WHOOP! WHOOP-WHOOP!*

When they hear it, they know they have sixteen minutes to get to class. That's not too difficult for those in Mr. Hardgroves's class on the third floor.

But Wayside School is a thirty-story building, with one room on each floor. So for those who happen to be in Mrs. Jewls's class, way up on the thirtieth floor, they must be ready on first *whoop*.

Todd was in Mrs. Jewls's class. He was stuck behind a mass of kids outside the building waiting for the doors to open. He jumped up and down, trying to see over the heads of those in front of him. If he was late, Mrs. Jewls would put his name on the blackboard, under the word DISCIPLINE.

The kids who went to class on the lower floors often dilly-dallied. If Todd got stuck behind a large group of dilly-dalliers, he'd have no chance.

Inside the principal's office, Mr. Kidswatter sat behind his enormous desk as he watched the clock. At the moment the second hand reached the number twelve, he shrieked into his microphone. *"WHOOP-WHOOP! WHOOP-WHOOP! WHOOP-WHOOP!"*

The doors unlocked, and the children stampeded into the building and up the stairs. Todd tried his best to weave his way to the front, but there wasn't a lot of room.

🍎 🍎 🍎

Eight minutes later, Mr. Kidswatter tugged on the rope hanging through the hole in the ceiling, and the second bell rang. *CLANG! CLANG! CLANG! CLANG! CLANG! CLANG! CLANG! CLANG!*

Todd counted the clangs. Eight. That meant he now had eight minutes to get to class. Seven or nine clangs would have meant something completely different. Seven meant a helicopter was landing on the roof. Nine clangs meant a porcupine had entered the building.

So far, he had only made it to the seventh floor, but he had finally managed to weave his way past all the dilly-dalliers. There was nothing to slow him down now.

When he reached the eighteenth floor, he heard this sound: *ching-a-ling, ching-a-ling, ching-a-ling.*

Nothing to worry about there. That just meant they were out of doughnuts in the teachers' lounge.

The scary bell was the late bell. It didn't matter where he was. It always sounded like an angry driver was slamming on a car horn, right behind him. It made Todd jump every time.

He quickly dashed from the eighteenth to the twentieth floor. There was no nineteenth floor.

His legs were sore, and he was breathing hard as he reached the top. Just ahead, he could see Joy entering the classroom.

"Don't shut the—" Todd shouted.

Joy shut the door behind her.

"Goozack," said Todd.

He was just opening it when the horn blared, as if right behind him.

"You're late, Todd," said Mrs. Jewls as he entered the classroom. "Write your—"

"I know," he said. He wrote his name on the blackboard, under the word DISCIPLINE.


Other bells rang throughout the day. At noon, the lunch bell kaboinked three times. Three kaboinks meant macaroons and cheese.

The bell for recess was just a single *ding*, but nobody ever missed it.

At the end of each day, Mr. Kidswatter would

bang a giant gong with a large iron mallet. It was his favorite thing about being principal.

Todd sat at his desk, glumly looking at the blackboard. The day had started off badly for him and had only gotten worse.

There was now a check mark next to his name, under the word DISCIPLINE.

Next to that, Mrs. Jewls kept adding new homework assignments.

READ A BOOK. WRITE A BOOK REPORT. DRAW A PICTURE.
(DON'T FORGET YOUR PAPER CLIP!!!)
HISTORY—READ PAGES 55-59 AND ANSWER QUESTIONS ON
PAGES 61 AND 62.
MATH WORKSHEET—DO EVEN- AND ODD-NUMBERED
PROBLEMS.
SCIENCE—READ PAGES 29-34, AND DO EXPERIMENT ON 37.

Todd had a sick feeling in his stomach, and it wasn't just the mac and cheese. In big letters, across the top of the blackboard, Mrs. Jewls had written:

ULTIMATE TEST STARTS TOMORROW!

Mrs. Jewls had been warning the class about the Ultimate Test all year. The test would last for three days. If he failed, Todd would be sent back to kindergarten.

And then he heard it—the most magical bell of all!

*Ping . . . PONG!*

This bell had only rung once in the history of Wayside School, and nobody knew who rang it. But everyone knew what it meant.

All around, kids began cheering and clapping their hands. Shouts of joy could be heard coming from every floor of Wayside School.

Todd just sat there, in stunned disbelief.

It rang again.

*Ping . . . PONG!*

It was the Erase-the-Blackboard bell.

Mrs. Jewls had no choice. She picked up the eraser. Up and down Wayside School, teachers were doing the same thing.

Todd smiled as the homework assignments were wiped away. The Ultimate Test was canceled. His name was removed from the discipline list, and even the word DISCIPLINE soon disappeared.

Deep in the basement, a man with a black mustache snapped open a black attaché case. Another man, also with a black mustache, placed a small silver ball into the case. A third man, who was bald, put in a solid gold Ping-Pong paddle.

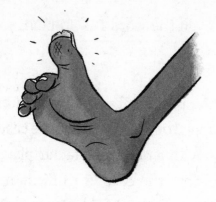

# 2

# A MILLION

By the time Terrence got to school, he had already kicked ninety-nine different things.

It started the moment he woke up. He kicked his bed. He kicked Rocky, his favorite stuffed animal. When he left his bedroom, he kicked the door shut.

He kicked the wall as he sat at the kitchen counter and ate cereal. He kicked a table. He kicked three chairs. He kicked rocks on the way to school. He kicked the flagpole.

Still, as much as Terrence liked to kick things, it would take him his whole life to kick a million things.

"How much is a million?" Mrs. Jewls asked her class.

"Ooh! Ooh! I know, I know!" said Mac, stretching his hand high.

Mrs. Jewls called on Mac.

"A million," Mac answered proudly.

"Well, yes, I suppose that's correct," said Mrs. Jewls. "A million is a million. Anyone else? John."

John lowered his hand. "Nine hundred and ninety-nine thousand, nine hundred and ninety-nine . . ." He paused, then added, "Plus one." He smiled.

"Ooh, that's good, John," said Dana, very impressed.

"John's really smart," Joe agreed.

Terrence wasn't paying attention. His big toe hurt from all that kicking. His toenail was too long.

Sharie, who had been sleeping at her desk,

suddenly awoke and said, "Ten times ten, times ten, times ten, times ten, times ten." She rested her head on her red-and-blue overcoat and went back to sleep.

"Is that right, Mrs. Jewls?" asked Jason.

"Um . . ." said Mrs. Jewls as she tried to multiply all of Sharie's tens. "Well, if Sharie said it, it must be right!"

"Arithmetic makes my brain numb," said Dameon.

"That's why they're called 'numb-ers,'" said D.J.

Terrence's big toe throbbed in pain. He couldn't think about anything else.

"There's really one way to understand just how big a million is," said Mrs. Jewls. "And it's not by using arithmetic. We need to collect a million *somethings*."

"Dollars!" exclaimed Joy.

Everyone cheered. They liked that idea.

"Then we could have the biggest party ever," said Deedee.

"We're not collecting a million dollars," said

Mrs. Jewls. "Any other ideas?"

"Pumpkins!" suggested Dana.

Everyone cheered Dana's idea too, but not as loudly as Joy's.

"I don't think a million pumpkins would fit in the school," said Mrs. Jewls. "We need something small, and not too expensive."

Stephen suggested, "Little pieces of paper."

Nobody cheered.

"Bo-ring," sang Kathy.

Stephen felt hurt, but deep down, he had to admit that collecting bits of paper wouldn't have been a whole lot of fun.

Ron suggested mud, but that too was rejected. "It's a good idea, Ron," said Mrs. Jewls, "but you can't count mud."

"Why not?" he asked.

"There's no such thing as one mud, or two muds," explained Mrs. Jewls.

"Why not?" Ron asked again.

"I don't know," Mrs. Jewls had to admit.

Terrence couldn't take it any longer. He took off his shoe, then his sock.

One desk over, Rondi stared at him, horrified.

Terrence's toenail was bent out of shape, and it had turned black and blue.

He opened his desk and took out his pair of safety scissors. Then, crossing one leg over the other, he started snipping.

"You can't cut your toenail in class," said Rondi. "It's against the rules."

"Who says?" said Terrence.

It was one tough toenail, and the scissors weren't all that sharp.

"Mrs. Jewls!" called Rondi. "Terrence is cutting his toenail, right in class!"

Some kids laughed. Some said, "Gross!"

Terrence pushed hard on the scissors. At last, a piece of his toenail fell free. His toe instantly felt better.

"Terrence! Come up here now!" demanded Mrs. Jewls. "And bring your toenail with you!"

Terrence picked up the clipping off the floor. One shoe off, one shoe on, he hobbled to the front of the room.

"Give me that!" Mrs. Jewls demanded.

Terrence dropped the nail clipping into his teacher's outstretched hand.

"You're a genius, Terrence," said Mrs. Jewls.

She held his nail clipping high in the air. "That's one!" she announced. "Nine hundred and ninety-nine thousand, nine hundred and ninety-nine . . . to go!"

# 3

## UP AND DOWN

"Up!" said D.J.

"Down!" replied Kathy, who sat next to him.

"Up!" D.J. repeated.

"Down!" Kathy insisted.

In truth, Kathy didn't know what D.J. was talking about. She just liked to argue. No matter what D.J. said, she always said the opposite.

"Up!" D.J. said again.

"Down!" Kathy instantly replied.

"Shh!" said Dana, who sat behind Kathy. "I'm trying to read."

Kathy turned around. Dana's face was streaked with tears.

"Why are you crying?" asked Kathy.

Dana showed her the book she'd been reading. *The Lost Giraffe.*

"So?" asked Kathy.

"The giraffe is lost," Dana sobbed.

"Well, what did you expect, stupid?" asked Kathy.

She didn't like Dana any more than she liked D.J.

"Up!" said D.J.

"Down!" snapped Kathy.

"Dana, Kathy, D.J.," said Mrs. Jewls. "You are making a lot of noise for silent reading."

"Sorry," said D.J. "I can't—up!—help it. I have the—up!—hiccups."

Kathy turned red. She had been arguing with a hiccup.

"Has this ever happened before?" Mrs. Jewls asked him.

"I've had the—up!—hiccups before," said D.J.,

"but they—up!—always went—up!—away."

"Stand on your head and drink a glass of water," Myron suggested.

"Eat a lemon," said Jenny.

"Hold your tongue while you say the Pledge of Allegiance," said Joy.

D.J. tried their suggestions. When he finished, his mouth was puckered, his shirt was wet, and he still had the hiccups.

He felt very patriotic, however.

"I think you better go see Dr. Pickle," said Mrs. Jewls. "Kathy will take you."

Kathy hopped out of her seat, glad she wouldn't have to read. "C'mon, dummy," she said, and led D.J. out the door.

"Up!" hiccuped D.J.

"Down!" said Kathy.

She couldn't help herself.


Dr. Pickle's real name was Dr. Pickell. His office was on the fourth floor. Kathy knocked on the door.

Dr. Pickle opened it. He had a pointy beard

16

and wore glasses. "Yes?" he said.

"Stupid here got the hiccups," said Kathy.

"Up!" hiccuped D.J.

"Down," said Kathy.

Dr. Pickle rubbed his chin. "Very interesting," he muttered, although he was looking at Kathy, not at D.J. "Very, very interesting."

He told Kathy to wait, and invited D.J. inside.

"And he smiles too much too!" Kathy called, just before the door shut.

D.J. sat down on a couch.

Dr. Pickle sat across from him. He held a long gold chain. On one end hung a green stone shaped like a pickle.

Dr. Pickle gently swung the stone, back and forth. "Watch the pickle," he said. His voice was warm and soothing.

D.J.'s eyes moved back and forth with the stone.

"I will count to five. And then you will fall into a deep, deep sleep." Dr. Pickle slowly counted. "One . . . two . . . BOO!"

D.J. fell off the couch.

"Well?" asked Dr. Pickle.

D.J. got up. He waited a moment. "I think they're gone," he said.

Dr. Pickle led him to the door. "First thing we learned in psychiatrist school," he said, patting D.J. on the head.

"My hiccups are all gone!" D.J. told Kathy.

"Who cares," said Kathy.

"Wait," said Dr. Pickle. "Would you mind stepping inside my office, young lady?"

"Me?" asked Kathy.

"Please," said Dr. Pickle.

"But he's the sicko!" said Kathy, pointing at D.J.

"Please," Dr. Pickle repeated.

Kathy shrugged, then entered the counselor's office. "That beard is really ugly," she said. "I guess your face must be even worse, huh?"

D.J. sat on the floor in the hallway, with his back against the wall, waiting for Kathy. He smiled, happy that his hiccups were gone. Although he missed them a little bit too. Hiccups are annoying, but kind of fun.

Some time later, the counselor's door opened.

"Thank you, Dr. Pickell," said Kathy, calling him by his proper name. "You are very wise. And I like your beard."

"That's very nice of you to say, Kathy," said the school counselor.

She stepped out the door. "Hi, D.J.," she greeted him. "Thanks for waiting. You're a good friend."

The smile left D.J.'s face. Something was definitely wrong with Kathy.

"Let's go up," said D.J.

"Yes, up," Kathy agreed.

Now he was really worried.

# 4

## CONSIDER THE PAPER CLIP

*Read a book. Write a book report. Draw a picture.*

That was the assignment Mrs. Jewls put up on the board.

Dana's picture showed a giraffe studying a map. She had drawn a large question mark over the giraffe's head.

Her book report only had to be one page, but she had written two whole pages. *The Lost Giraffe* was her favorite book ever!

Now all she needed was a paper clip.

She searched her desk.

She found quite a few pencils, mostly broken. There were lots of eraser bits and crayon nubs. There was also a crumb-covered pink piece of paper that had come off the bottom of a cupcake.

"Oh no, oh no, oh no," she moaned as she continued to search.

She raised her hand.

"Yes, Dana," said Mrs. Jewls.

"I need a new paper clip."

"But I gave you one at the beginning of the year," said Mrs. Jewls.

"I know, Mrs. Jewls. I'm sorry. I just can't find it!"

Mrs. Jewls sighed. "I'm very disappointed in you, Dana."

"I need a paper clip too," said Joe.

Mrs. Jewls glared at him. "What did you do with the one I gave you?" she demanded.

"I think I used it on my science homework," said Joe.

"I handed that back yesterday," Mrs. Jewls

reminded him. "Didn't you save the paper clip?"

"I guess not," Joe admitted.

Bebe was finishing up the last part of her picture. "Paper clip, please," she said, without looking up from her work.

"One for me too," said Calvin.

Mrs. Jewls slammed her hand on her desk. "Do you think paper clips grow on trees?" she asked.

"I don't know," said Calvin.

"I gave each one of you a paper clip at the beginning of the year. It was your responsibility to take care of it." She opened her desk drawer, took out her paper clip box, and opened it. "There are only six left," she said, shaking her head in dismay.

"Ooh, can I have one?" asked Joy. "I can't find mine."

Mrs. Jewls was too angry to reply. She moved to the front of the room. "You children are so spoiled," she said. "Do you have any idea what it takes to make just one paper clip?"

She held up one of her last remaining paper clips. "Look at the perfect double loop. And the way it gleams in the light, almost like a mirror."

Her anger seemed to melt away as she marveled at the magnificent metal masterpiece.

"It takes a lot of very talented people, and years of training and hard work," she explained. "First, there's the wire maker. Paper clip wire has to be just right, not too stiff, but not too wiggly either.

"Then there's the wire polisher," she continued. "That's who gives the paper clip its special gleam. And the wire cutter, who cuts each wire to the precise length.

"And finally, and most important, the master bender. The bender carefully bends the wire into the perfect double loop." She put her hand over her heart. "Sadly, in these rush-rush, hurry-hurry days, not too many young people study the art of paper clip bending. There are only a handful of master benders left in the whole world. And who knows, in ten or twenty years there might not be any. Everyone will have to switch to staples."

"That is so sad," said Dana.

Mrs. Jewls gave the paper clip to Dana. "Now don't lose it!"

"I won't!" Dana promised.

"Let me see," said Bebe.

Dana proudly showed Bebe her new paper clip.

"It's so beautiful!" said Bebe, admiring the double loops. "I never noticed before."

"I'm going to be a paper clip bender when I grow up," said Calvin.

Mrs. Jewls smiled at Calvin. She had never been more proud of a student.

# 5

## ERIC, ERIC, AND *WHAT'S-HIS-NAME?*

Oh, that's right—Eric.

There are three Erics in Mrs. Jewls's class: Eric Fry, Eric Bacon, and the other one—who everyone always forgets—Eric Ovens.

Eric Fry is strong and fast. He is usually the first one chosen when picking teams.

Eric Bacon is funny, clever, and just a little bit sneaky. Everyone in Mrs. Jewls's class likes him, but no one completely trusts him.

Eric Ovens is kind, quiet, and 100 percent trustworthy. Sadly, that kind of person is often overlooked.

But not today, he thought as he sat at his desk, patiently waiting for Mrs. Jewls to finish taking attendance. Today would be his day of glory!

In his pocket was a plastic bag with eighty-three nail clippings!

Two numbers had been written on the blackboard: 71 and 2,677.

So far, the class had collected a total of 2,677 nail clippings. Seventy-one were the most brought in by any one kid.

They didn't just have to be toenails. Finger-nails counted too.

Eric Ovens took his bag out of his pocket and placed it on his desk.

"How many you got?" whispered Kathy, who sat next to him.

Eric didn't want to jinx his big day by saying the number aloud. Besides, he knew Kathy would only say something mean, or mock him.

Mrs. Jewls closed her attendance book. "Anyone have any nail clippings this morning?"

Eric Ovens raised his hand.

"Yes, Eric," said Mrs. Jewls.

Eric Ovens quietly pushed his chair back, but before he could get up, he saw Eric Fry already making his way to the front of the room.

"Forty!" Eric Fry declared proudly.

Eric Fry had kept his hand in a fist all morning. Everyone thought he was just trying to be tough. Now he opened his fist and let forty nail clippings fall into the collection bucket.

"Well done, Eric!" said Mrs. Jewls.

Everyone clapped their hands.

Eric Ovens smiled as he clapped his hands too. Eighty-three was more than double forty.

Eric Fry did the math on the board.

$$
\begin{array}{r}
2677 \\
+\ 40 \\
\hline
2717
\end{array}
$$

"Halfway to a million!" cheered Stephen.

"Not quite," Allison told him.

"Anyone else?" asked Mrs. Jewls.

Again Eric Ovens raised his hand, but Eric

Bacon had already hopped out of his seat and was headed toward the front of the room.

He handed Mrs. Jewls a plastic bag full of nail clippings. "Three hundred and forty-nine!" he declared triumphantly.

The class went wild. Sharie gasped. Stephen fell out of his chair.

Eric Bacon danced around Mrs. Jewls's desk, like a football player who had scored a touchdown.

Mrs. Jewls was skeptical of the spectacle. "I could count them," she warned.

Eric stopped dancing. "Go ahead," he challenged her.

Mrs. Jewls stared Eric Bacon in the eye. Eric Bacon stared right back.

Mrs. Jewls dumped the bag on her desk, and divided the clippings into four piles. She asked Dameon, Allison, and John to help. They each took a pile, and then Mrs. Jewls added their totals together.

"Three hundred and forty-nine," she announced, "just as Eric said."

Again, everyone cheered, and Eric Bacon

continued his victory dance.

"How did you get so many?" Mrs. Jewls asked him.

Eric B. stopped dancing. "I went door-to-door, asking my neighbors," he said.

Everyone laughed.

Leslie had sold wrapping paper door-to-door, but she couldn't imagine asking people for their toenails!

"It's easier than asking for money," said Eric. "Everyone was happy to donate."

He erased the number 71 and put 349 in its place. Then he did the math.

$$\begin{array}{r} 2717 \\ + 349 \\ \hline 3066 \end{array}$$

"Almost a million!" Stephen called out.

"Not even close," muttered Allison.

Mrs. Jewls told Eric Bacon to take a Tootsie Roll Pop from her coffee can.

He took one. Then, when she wasn't looking, he took another.

"Anyone else?" asked Mrs. Jewls.

Eric Ovens sat glumly at his desk.

"Raise your hand," urged Kathy.

"Why bother?" he muttered.

Kathy got up from her seat and stood next to him. She grabbed Eric's arm and raised it for him. "Eric Ovens brought a whole lot!" she announced.

"Bring them on up," said Mrs. Jewls.

He had no choice. "It's just eighty-three," he said, and then emptied his bag into the nail bucket.

"That's the second most ever!" shouted Kathy. She started clapping.

Amazingly, everyone else clapped too.

They were still clapping as he did the math on the board.

$$3066$$
$$\underline{+\ 83}$$
$$3149$$

"That's closer to a million!" exclaimed Stephen.

Everyone cheered.

Even Allison couldn't argue with that.

# 6

## OPPOSITOSIS

Eric Ovens wasn't the only one who had noticed that Kathy had become nice. Others, too, began to notice her odd behavior.

"I like your picture," Kathy told Bebe.

"What's wrong with it?" Bebe asked.

"Nothing," said Kathy. "It's perfect. You are very talented."

It took Bebe a moment to realize that Kathy hadn't insulted her.

Mrs. Jewls also noticed the change. "Kathy, will you come here, please?" she asked.

Kathy approached her teacher's desk. "Yes, Mrs. Jewls?" she asked.

Mrs. Jewls smiled. "You have been doing very well, Kathy," she said. "I've noticed a real improvement in your work, *and* in your attitude."

"That must be because you're such a good teacher," said Kathy.

"Well, thank you," said Mrs. Jewls. "But there's a tiny little problem. I'm having a hard time reading your homework."

"What do you mean?"

"Look at it," said Mrs. Jewls, showing Kathy her most recent homework assignment.

"What's wrong with it?" asked Kathy.

@ @ @

"First thing we learned in psychiatrist school," Dr. Pickle said as he patted D.J. on the head.

"My hiccups are all gone!" D.J. told Kathy.

"Who cares," Kathy grumpled.

"Would you mind stepping inside my office, young lady?" asked Dr. Pickle.

"But he's the sicko!" said Kathy, pointing at D.J.

"Please," said Dr. Pickle.

She entered the counselor's office. "That beard is really ugly. I guess your face must be even worse, huh?"

Dr. Pickle didn't get angry. He just stroked his beard and said, "Very interesting."

Kathy sniffed. "Smells like pickles," she commented.

"Very interesting, indeed," the counselor said, and then asked her to sit down.

Kathy sat on the couch. "Lumpy," she complained.

"I'm going to try a little experiment," said Dr. Pickle. "I'm going to say a word, and then I want you to say the first word that pops into your head."

"Stupid!" said Kathy.

"I haven't started yet," said Dr. Pickle.

"Sloppy!" said Kathy.

Dr. Pickle realized he had better hurry up and get started. "Cold," he began.

"Hot," Kathy replied.

"Hard."

"Soft."

"Skinny."

"Fat."

"This is kind of fun, isn't it, Kathy?" asked Dr. Pickle.

"No, it's boring," said Kathy.

"Worse than I thought," said Dr. Pickle. "I studied your condition in psychiatrist school. "I'm afraid you have a bad case of oppositosis."

"No, I don't. You do!"

Dr. Pickle stroked his beard.

Unfortunately, there was no known cure for oppositosis. Other psychiatrists had tried to help their patients learn to be kind and think positively.

Dr. Pickle knew that would never work on Kathy. He had his own theory, however. He could try to turn her opposites into double opposites.

He opened his desk drawer and took out his pickle-stone and chain.

Kathy watched the green stone as it gently swung back and forth. She fell asleep on the count of five.

"Can you hear me, Kathy?" he asked.

"And I can smell you too," she replied.

"You are looking into a mirror," he told her.

"I'm looking into a mirror," Kathy repeated, eyes closed.

"Tell me what you see."

"I see a beautiful girl with black hair," she said. "And I see a funny-looking man with a pointy beard."

"Very good," said Dr. Pickle. "Now I want you to reach out and touch the mirror."

Kathy slowly moved her arm.

"But as you try to touch it," said Dr. Pickle, "you'll discover the mirror isn't solid. Your hand will go right through it."

Kathy stuck her hand out farther. "That's weird," she said.

"Now stand up, and walk through the mirror."

Kathy stood up. She took one step, then another. She hesitated for a moment, and then took one last step.

"Amazing!" she exclaimed.

"You are on the other side of the mirror," said Dr. Pickle. "What do you see?"

Kathy looked around. "Nice office," she said. She sniffed. "Smells nice too."

"I'm glad you like it," said Dr. Pickle. "Would you like to sit on the couch?"

Kathy sat back down. "Very comfortable," she noted.

"When I count to three, you will wake up. But you will still be on the other side of the mirror. One . . . two . . . three."

Kathy opened her eyes.

"How do you feel?" he asked her.

"Fine, thanks," said Kathy. "How are you?"

"Very well, thank you," said Dr. Pickle. "Do you mind if we continue with our little experiment?"

"Sounds like fun," said Kathy.

"Happy," said Dr. Pickle.

"Smile," said Kathy.

"Smart," said Dr. Pickle.

"Mrs. Jewls," said Kathy.

"Friend," said Dr. Pickle.

"D.J.," said Kathy.

Dr. Pickle led her to the door.

"Thank you, Dr. Pickell," she said, shaking his hand. "You are very wise. And I like your beard."

ⓢ ⓢ ⓢ

"What's wrong with my homework?" asked Kathy.

"It's written backward!" said Mrs. Jewls. "Every sentence. Every word. Every letter. Even the numbers are backward."

"Looks normal to me," said Kathy. "Do you want me to do it over?"

Mrs. Jewls sighed. "No, that's all right, Kathy. I'm just happy to see you doing so well. I'll figure it out."

Kathy smiled, and then returned to her seat.

# 7

# THE CLOSET
# THAT WASN'T THERE

Mac was a curious kid.

When Miss Mush served chicken fingers, he asked her how many fingers a chicken had on each hand.

After lunch, he played basketball. Besides playing, he was also the self-appointed announcer, describing every shot, every pass, and every dribble.

Jenny finally told him to put a sock in it.

Only then, when he stopped talking, did Mac remember that he'd left his catcher's mask in the cafeteria. Mac liked to wear his catcher's mask for all sports, including basketball.

He was a curious kid.

The cafeteria was on the fifteenth floor. Mac found his mask right where he'd left it, but by then, it hardly seemed worth it to go all the way back down to the playground. So he continued on up to the thirtieth story.

And there, just outside his classroom door, was the most curious thing that Mac had ever seen. Next to the wall was some sort of giant closet. It hadn't been there before lunch.

But that wasn't what made it curious. The closet was wrapped up in heavy chains, and locked with a giant padlock.

Mac moved closer. Behind the chains, he could see double doors, with a steel bar clamped across them. Several signs were taped to the doors.

"KEEP BACK!"

"DO NOT OPEN DOORS!"

"DANGER!"

"CALL THE FIRE DEPARTMENT IF YOU SMELL SOMETHING UNUSUAL!"

Mac sniffed, but all he could smell were chicken fingers.

Behind the chains, and the steel bar, each door had its own lock. He could see two keyholes, one red and the other green.

He put on his catcher's mask, just to be safe, and tried to open one door, then the other. They wouldn't budge.

He tried to peer through the keyholes, but they were too tiny.

He knocked on one of the doors. It seemed to be made of thick wood. "Anyone in there?" he called.

There was no answer. He knocked again, and then pressed his ear against the side of the closet.

Still nothing.

"What's that?" asked Deedee, coming up the stairs.

Mac shrugged.

Deedee read the signs aloud. "Keep back. Do not open doors. Danger."

She tried one of the doors.

"I think it's locked," said Mac.

More kids made it up the stairs. Each one stopped at the closet, read the signs, and then tried to open the doors.

Terrence kicked the doors.

Jason rattled the chains. "Look, it's one long chain," he determined, "wrapped around four times."

"What do you think is inside?" asked Leslie.

"Snakes," said Paul. He was afraid of snakes.

"Spiders," said Rondi. She was afraid of spiders.

"Monsters," said Allison.

She loved monsters.

"What if it's Mrs. Gorf?" guessed Calvin.

Everyone shuddered.

Mrs. Gorf was the worst teacher they'd ever had.

"Give me a boost," said Mac.

Jenny cupped her hands, and Mac stepped up,

first onto Jenny's hands, then onto the steel bar. He gripped the top edge of the closet and tried to shimmy up.

"Get away from there!" shouted Mrs. Jewls. "All of you!"

She had returned from the teachers' lounge only to see the children hanging all over the closet, like monkeys.

"Mac, get down, now!"

Mac tried to hop down, but his foot got tangled in the chains, and he fell onto his back.

"Ooh, I think I broke my tailbone," he complained.

"You're lucky that's all you broke!" said Mrs. Jewls.

"What's inside?" asked Terrence.

"Never you mind!" said Mrs. Jewls. "Don't you children know the meaning of DANGER? You are not to go anywhere near my closet! Don't look at it. Don't even think about it. It's not there!"

"But I can see it," said Mac, still lying on the floor.

"It's Not There!" Mrs. Jewls insisted.

"But—"

"No Ifs, Ands, or Buts!" said Mrs. Jewls.

Everyone shuffled inside the classroom.

Mac was still on the floor. He stood up and adjusted his catcher's mask, which had become cockeyed when he fell. He took one last look at the closet that wasn't there, then walked into the classroom, more curious than ever.

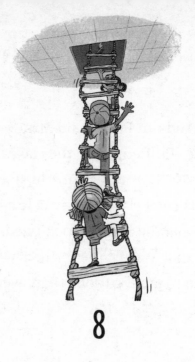

# 8

## SCIENCE

Twenty-nine hands were raised.

There were only twenty-eight kids in Mrs. Jewls's class, but Joy stretched both her arms high in the air. She figured it doubled her chance of being chosen. She waved them back and forth, and around in circles.

"Pick me, pick me!" begged Bebe.

"Pick me, Mrs. Jewls," urged Calvin, sitting next to Bebe.

"Sorry, Calvin, you're too heavy," Mrs. Jewls told him. "And your toes are too tiny, Bebe."

Todd sat behind Joy but Mrs. Jewls couldn't see him behind Joy's helicopter arms.

"Okay, Joy!" said Mrs. Jewls.

Everyone else groaned.

Joy was all smiles. "You lose, losers!" she said as she headed toward the door.

This week, for science, they would be studying clouds. Luckily, Mrs. Jewls's class was on the thirtieth floor. It was the classroom closest to the sky.

Last week, they studied dirt. That wasn't so lucky. By the time they made it down to the ground, science was over, and they had to turn around and trudge back up.

Everyone brought their science notebooks and gathered just outside the door, by the closet that wasn't there.

Mrs. Jewls put her hands around Joy's waist. "Alley-oopsy!" she called out, and lifted Joy straight up.

Joy giggled.

This was why Mrs. Jewls hadn't chosen Calvin.

He was too heavy for her to lift.

Mrs. Jewls set Joy on top of the closet. Just above her, a trapdoor led to the roof. Joy stood on her tiptoes and pushed it open. This was why Mrs. Jewls hadn't chosen Bebe. Her toes weren't long enough.

A rope ladder tumbled down.

One by one, the children climbed the rope ladder to the roof.

"Be sure to stay away from the edge," Mrs. Jewls called up to them.

There was a safety railing around the edge, but it was for taller people. Mrs. Jewls was afraid her students could slip right under it.

She was the last one up through the trapdoor. When she reached the roof, she saw everyone standing at the edge.

"What did I just say?" she demanded.

Everyone stared blankly at her.

"Alley-oopsy?" asked Dameon.

"Well, at least somebody was paying attention," said Mrs. Jewls. She told everyone to take two steps back, and to sit on their bottoms.

"But then we'll be farther away from the clouds," Mac complained.

"Sometimes, safety is more important," said Mrs. Jewls.

She pointed out the clouds to her class. "That one there is a cumulus cloud."

Some of the students wrote it down in their notebooks. Bebe drew a picture of a sleeping giant. The cumulus cloud was his pillow.

"And that's a cirrus cloud over there," said Mrs. Jewls.

Bebe drew a picture of flying angels. Hundreds of white feathers had fallen from their wings and had swirled into a cloud.

Bebe could draw really fast.

"What kind of cloud is that one, Mrs. Jewls?" asked Benjamin.

He was pointing at a dull, dark cloud way off in the distance.

Mrs. Jewls gasped.

If Bebe were to draw it, her picture would look exactly like the inside of a vacuum cleaner bag, while the vacuum was still on.

But Bebe had never seen the inside of a vacuum cleaner bag while the vacuum was still on. So she couldn't draw it.

"Everyone back to the classroom!" Mrs. Jewls shouted. "Double quick!"

The children scrambled to the trapdoor.

"Hurry!" ordered Mrs. Jewls.

Some fell right through. Others got rope burns.

Mrs. Jewls didn't worry about little things like that.

She was the last one through the hatch. Sitting atop the closet that wasn't there, she tossed the ladder back on the roof and locked the trapdoor.

She climbed down, stepping onto the chains and steel bar.

The children were waiting quietly inside the classroom, hands folded on their desks.

Mrs. Jewls walked to the side of the room and looked out the window. Either the cloud was moving closer, or it was getting bigger.

Or both.

"What kind of cloud is it, Mrs. Jewls?" asked Leslie.

There are times when adults hide the truth from children, so as not to worry them. But Mrs. Jewls was a teacher. And this was science.

"Take a good look, boys and girls," she said, pointing out the window. Then, with a slight tremble in her voice, she said, "That is a Cloud of Doom."

The room darkened.

# 9

# THE GONNNNNG

Louis, the yard teacher, was filling a green ball with air when the Cloud of Doom cast its gloomy shadow over the schoolyard. He felt an eerie chill as he pushed down on his air pump.

Suddenly there was a loud *BANG*, and the next thing Louis knew, he was lying on the blacktop.

He slowly sat up. He wiggled his fingers. He stuck out his tongue and moved it from side to side. He seemed to be okay. He stood up, still a little wobbly.

Bits of green rubber were scattered across the playground. His air pump was on the other side of the dodgeball circle.

The ball must have exploded from too much air, he realized.

He always tried to put the maximum amount of air into each ball. The kids liked them bouncy. The bouncier the better.

He picked up a piece of green rubber. Then another. And another.

There already weren't enough balls to go around. The school couldn't afford to lose another one. He'd have to sew it back together.

In the end he found seventy-three pieces. It was unusually dark for this time of day. He hoped he hadn't missed any.

"The gong!" he remembered. He hurried to the principal's office, stuffing cotton balls into his ears as he ran.

"You're late, Louis," said Mr. Kidswatter, but Louis couldn't hear him.

He wheeled the giant gong out of the office to the bottom of the stairs.

At one time, the gong had been bright and shiny, but that was before Louis's time. Now it was dull and heavily dented. A large mallet, also made of iron, hung from a hook bolted to the gong's wood frame.

Louis unhooked it, and then took a couple of steps backward to steady himself. The mallet was heavy, even for someone as strong as the yard teacher.

He handed it to Mr. Kidswatter, who easily raised it over his shoulder. Mr. Kidswatter had thick arms, a thick neck, and a thick head.

Louis started the countdown. "Ten . . . nine . . . eight . . ."

There was a red dot in the center of the gong. On the count of "One!" Mr. Kidswatter swung the mallet and hit it dead center.

*GONNNNN-nnnnn-NNNNN-nnnnn-NNN-NN-nnnnn-NNNNN . . .*

Despite the cotton balls, the sound rattled inside Louis's head, and echoed up and down the stairs.

*...nnnnn-NNNNN-nnnnn-NNNNN-nnnnn...*

Louis took the mallet from Mr. Kidswatter and hung it back on its hook. He wheeled the gong off to the side, just before a river of children flooded down the stairs.

"Hi, Louis!" "Bye, Louis! "See you tomorrow, Louis!" they called to him as they ran by.

He smiled and waved, but all he heard was "Gonnnnnng!"

"Why don't they ever say those things to me?" Mr. Kidswatter asked a little while later, as they were leaving the school together.

"Maybe if you did something nice?" Louis suggested.

"Like what?" asked the principal.

"Maybe let a kid ring the gong?"

"No way," snapped Mr. Kidswatter. "That's the best part about being principal."

"Or how about getting some more balls for recess?" Louis suggested.

"Too expensive," said Mr. Kidswatter.

"What if I pay for them?" asked Louis.

Mr. Kidswatter laughed. "You? Where would

you get that kind of money? Did you rob a bank?"

"I have money," said Louis. "I've written some books about Wayside School."

"And you got paid for that?" Mr. Kidswatter asked.

Louis shrugged.

Mr. Kidswatter frowned.

Louis hoped he hadn't broken a law.

"Do you mention me in the books?" asked Mr. Kidswatter.

"Maybe once or twice," Louis admitted.

"You don't say anything bad about me, do you?"

"Ummm . . ." said Louis.

"You should write a chapter about me!" declared Mr. Kidswatter. "Call it 'The Best Principal Ever!!!' with three exclamation points."

"First, you would have to do something that makes you the best principal ever," Louis explained.

"Like what?"

"Let a kid ring the gong."

This time, Mr. Kidswatter didn't snap at Louis.

He was thinking about it.

Louis looked up at the gloomy cloud. He hadn't paid much attention to science, back when he was going to school. He didn't know it was a Cloud of Doom.

Had he known, he never would have made such a dangerous suggestion to Mr. Kidswatter.

# 10

## STUCK

Everybody has a special talent. Bebe can draw. Joe can stand on his head and sing "Jingle Bells."

But this story isn't about Bebe or Joe. It's about Dana.

Dana can make funny faces.

Just by puffing out one cheek and raising the opposite eyebrow, she can make Jenny and Leslie crack up every time.

Or there's the one she calls her goofball face.

She puts her glasses on upside down. Then she pulls down one corner of her mouth with her pinky finger, while with her other hand, she tugs her earlobe.

When Dameon and Myron saw that one, they laughed so hard they bumped heads.

Even Mrs. Jewls laughs at Dana's funny faces. "But you need to be careful, Dana," she warned. "You don't want your face to get stuck that way."

Dana wasn't worried about that. No matter how weirdly she stretched it, her face always bounced back.

But that was before the Cloud of Doom settled over the school. It had been there a week now, even as other clouds drifted past. Each day, it seemed to grow a little bit larger.

Dana and Leslie were on the playground, waiting for Jenny. It was recess, and Jenny went to get "Patches" from Louis.

"Patches" was the ball that Louis had blown up, in more ways than one.

Louis never found all the pieces, and had to cut up an old yellow raincoat to fill in the gaps. Jenny, Leslie, and Dana liked Patches the best, because it was impossible to predict which way it would bounce.

"Hey, Dana, there's a giant worm on your foot!" said John.

Dana looked down at her sneaker.

"Made you look!" John exclaimed. He and Joe laughed.

"So she looked at her foot?" asked Leslie. "What's wrong with that?"

"There wasn't even a worm!" explained Joe.

Dana felt like a big doofus. Why did she always fall for John's tricks?

She made her Doofus Face.

She closed her right eye, raised her left eyebrow, puffed out her right cheek, and stuck out her tongue.

When John looked at it, he suddenly felt like a big doofus. "Sorry," he muttered. "It was just a dumb joke."

He hung his head and walked away. Joe followed.

Dana felt sad for John. She hadn't meant to call him a doofus. She had just wanted to make him laugh. She liked it when John teased her.

Jenny returned with Patches.

"You missed it!" said Leslie. "Dana got back at John good!"

Jenny turned to Dana. "Why are you calling me a doofus?" she asked.

Dana didn't realize she was still wearing her Doofus Face. She tried to pull her tongue back in but it wouldn't budge. Her cheek wouldn't unpuff. Her right eye remained shut, and her left eyebrow stayed up.

"That's not nice," said Jenny.

"Uhhhhh . . ." said Dana.

"Oh my gosh!" exclaimed Leslie. "Is your face stuck?"

Dana nodded. Her Doofus Face moved up and down.

"So you're not doing it on purpose?" asked Jenny.

Her Doofus Face turned right, then left.

"It's the Cloud of Doom!" exclaimed Jenny.

Leslie covered her mouth with her hand.

The three girls looked up at the dark and swirling cloud.

"I'll get Louis," Leslie said, and hurried away.

She returned with the yard teacher a short while later.

Louis laughed when he saw Dana.

"It's her Doofus Face," said Jenny.

"It's a good one," said Louis. "I think I like it even better than your Goofball Face."

"But now her face is stuck that way!" said Leslie.

Louis thought a moment, and then blew his whistle real loud. Jenny and Leslie covered their ears.

Dana's face remained stuck.

Louis didn't really expect it to work. He just liked blowing his whistle.

Kids from all over the playground came running at the sound of it.

"What's up, Louis?" asked Todd.

"Dana's face is stuck," Jenny explained.

"Really?" asked Todd. He poked Dana's puffed-out cheek. It was like poking a rock.

Mr. Kidswatter also heard the whistle. "Out of my way, let me through," he ordered as he made his way to Louis and Dana. "What's going on here?" he demanded.

He looked at Dana.

Dana looked back at Mr. Kidswatter.

Their eyes locked.

It became a staring contest. Everyone wondered who would blink first.

But Dana couldn't blink.

Finally, Mr. Kidswatter turned away. "Cute kid," he said, and patted Dana on the head. He headed back to the building.

Dana's face instantly popped back into place.

"Your face is fixed!" exclaimed Jenny.

Dana smiled, but then she made her face return to just plain normal. She didn't want her smile to get stuck. Even that could be unpleasant. As long as they were under the Cloud of Doom, she would have to be very careful with her facial expressions.

Mr. Kidswatter walked quickly back to his office. He shut the door behind him.

He was sticking out his tongue. His left eye was shut tight, his right eyebrow was raised, and his left cheek was all puffed out.

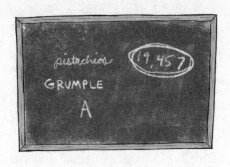

# 11

## WHAT'S THE POINT?

In some classrooms, teachers choose the weekly spelling words. Not so in Mrs. Jewls's class. She lets her students pick.

Nearly everyone had a hand raised. Mrs. Jewls called on Rondi.

"Pistachios," said Rondi.

This is why other teachers don't let their students choose the words. Mrs. Jewls couldn't spell *pistachios*.

So she did what every teacher everywhere does in such situations. "That's an excellent word, Rondi," she said. "Would you like to come up and write it on the board?"

Rondi came to the front of the room. Mrs. Jewls paid close attention as Rondi wrote *pistachios* on the blackboard.

"I love pistachios," said Kathy when Rondi returned to her seat.

"Me too," said Allison. "They're my third-favorite nut."

Mrs. Jewls called on D.J.

"Grumple," he said.

"I don't think 'grumple' is a word," Mrs. Jewls pointed out.

"So?" asked D.J. "We should still know how to spell it."

"It might become a word someday," Kathy agreed.

Mrs. Jewls wrote *grumple* under *pistachios*.

Joy raised her hand. "A," she suggested.

"*A what?*" asked Mrs. Jewls.

"Just a," said Joy.

"Don't you think that's a little too easy?"

said Mrs. Jewls.

"It's a very common word," said Kathy. "It's important that we all know how to spell it."

Mrs. Jewls couldn't argue with that. She added *a* to the list.

Myron had his hand raised.

"Yes, Myron," said Mrs. Jewls.

"What's the point?" Myron asked.

"That's three words," said Mrs. Jewls.

"And all good ones too," chirped Kathy.

"The Cloud of Doom is getting bigger every day!" Myron exclaimed. "What does it matter if we can spell?"

"So we can read and write," Mrs. Jewls replied.

"What's the point of reading?" asked Leslie.

"What's the point of writing?" asked Jason.

"What the point of arithmetic?" asked Benjamin.

"There is no point!" Myron grumpled. He slammed his pencil down hard on his desk. The point broke off of it.

"I understand you're scared and upset," said Mrs. Jewls. "But *what's the point* of quitting? We can all just sit around and grumple, or we can try to do our best, cloud or no cloud.

"And it hasn't been all bad," Mrs. Jewls continued. "We've been getting a whole lot more nail clippings."

That was true. Ever since the Cloud of Doom appeared, everyone's fingernails and toenails had been growing a lot faster. They had to be clipped three or four times a week.

The number on the board was now 19,457.

"Someday, the Cloud of Doom will be gone," said Mrs. Jewls. "And the world will be a much better place, even better than before the cloud. Colors will be more colorful. Music will be more musical. Even Miss Mush's food will taste good. The bigger the storm, the brighter the rainbow."

At that moment, a crack of thunder shook the classroom, and then the lights went out.

The children screamed. They weren't scared. They just liked screaming in the dark.

Mrs. Jewls lit a candle, and everyone settled down. "Now, shall we continue with our spelling?"

Jenny raised her hand and suggested, "Hope."

"Excellent word," said Mrs. Jewls.

She held her candle in one hand, and the chalk in the other. She said the letters out loud as she wrote them on the blackboard.

"H-o-p-e."

# 12

## MRS. SURLAW

The library was on the seventh floor. Mrs. Surlaw was the librarian.

A giant stuffed walrus sat next to her desk.
The walrus was bigger than most of the kids in
the school, and a couple of the teachers too.

Kindergarteners often got scared the first
time they saw Mrs. Surlaw's walrus. When they
dared touch one of its giant tusks, however, they
discovered it was soft as a pillow.

There were lots of rules in the library. No eating, no drinking, no yelling, no somersaults, and no hugging the walrus until after you checked out a book.

Mrs. Surlaw wheeled her book cart along a row of bookcases. She picked up a book, turned to the last page, and then put it on the shelf where it belonged. She took another book, checked its last page, and put that one in its proper place as well.

She heard the rumble of feet on the stairs, and the chirps and shrieks of young voices. This was followed by shushing sounds.

Mrs. Jewls's class politely entered the library. They were scared of Mrs. Surlaw.

While the two adults greeted each other, the children scurried to different parts of the library. They had only fifteen minutes to choose and check out a book.

"Have you read *The Pig, the Princess, and the Potato*?" Leslie asked Jenny.

"Is it good?"

"Only the best book ever!"

Mrs. Surlaw smiled when she heard that. The

only thing she loved more than books were children who loved books. She may have seemed severe on the outside, but inside, her heart was soft as a pillow.

Some libraries have separate areas for fiction and nonfiction. Mrs. Surlaw didn't believe in that sort of thing. After all, who was she to decide what was true and what wasn't?

She also didn't believe in alphabetical order.

Her books were organized by number of pages. Skinny books were at one end of the library, and the fat ones were at the opposite end.

Along the shelves were number markers: 10, 20, 30 . . . all the way to 1,000. If someone in Mrs. Jewls's class wanted to read this book, he or she could find it between the 180 and 190 markers.

Joy was looking through the books between the 40 and 50 markers. She had already read every book in the library with fewer than forty pages.

Allison liked long novels. She was looking through the ones that were between 230 and 240 pages.

Jason stood behind her, watching.

At last, Allison chose her book. It had 232 pages.

Jason took the one next to it, with 233 pages.

Allison scowled at him. She put her book back, and then chose one farther down the shelf, with 238 pages.

Jason put his book back too. He took one with 239 pages.

Allison pretended not to notice, even though she was burning inside. She looked at her book. "I think I already read this," she said aloud. She returned it to the shelf. "La-di-da," she said. "What book do I want to read?"

Suddenly she dashed to the end of the aisle, and around a corner.

Jason had trouble squeezing his book back into place. By the time he did, he couldn't see Allison anywhere.

He went from one end of the library to the other, searching between the aisles. When he finally saw her, she was hugging the walrus. That meant she had already checked out her book.

He went to her. "Hey, Allison," he said. "Can I see your book?"

"No," she replied.

"How many pages?" he asked.

"I'm not telling you."

"More than three hundred?"

"Maybe."

"No way," he said. "Even you wouldn't read a book with more than three hundred pages."

Allison shrugged.

"More than three hundred and fifty?" he asked.

"Maybe."

"Five hundred?"

"Maybe."

"Just tell me the title."

"No!"

"I'm just trying to help you," he explained. "Maybe I've already read it. I could tell you if it's any good. You don't want to read a five-hundred-page book if it's boring, or has a bunch of kissing in it."

Rondi finished checking out her book, and

then hugged the walrus too.

"Let's go, Rondi," said Allison.

Jason watched the two girls leave the library.

He went to Mrs. Surlaw. "How many pages in Allison's book?" he asked.

"I'm sorry, Jason," the librarian told him. "That is confidential information."

Jason sighed.

He returned to the bookshelves, wondering if Allison really chose a book with five hundred pages. It seemed impossible. Nobody could read a book that long, even if it had big print and short chapters.

Still he couldn't be sure. Just to be safe, he chose a book with 510 pages. There was no way Allison chose a longer book than that! He started to bring it to Mrs. Surlaw.

*But what if she did?*

He put the book back, then found one with 573 pages. She couldn't have chosen a book with more pages than that!

Again, he started to Mrs. Surlaw's desk.

*But what if she did?*

He returned the book to its place on the shelf,

and then chose one with 611 pages. A moment later he returned it.

No matter which book he chose, the same question kept returning.

*But what if she did?*

Finally, Jason chose the last book, on the last shelf, at the very end of the library. He had to hold it with both hands as he lugged it to the checkout desk.

The number on its last page was 999. The book made a loud thud as he plopped it down on the desk.

"Excellent choice, Jason!" Mrs. Surlaw said when she saw the book. "I know you will enjoy reading it."

*Reading it?* He couldn't even carry it.

Jason hugged the walrus.

# 13

## UMBRELLA

Sharie liked walking in the rain. She liked stomping through puddles in her yellow rain boots. Most of all, she loved her umbrella, even if it did get heavy after a while.

Her umbrella was purple with green stripes. Or maybe it was green with purple stripes. She couldn't be sure. The whole thing was covered with yellow polka dots of various sizes.

She liked listening to the raindrops bounce off of it. The harder it rained, the better the sound. She liked the feel of the smooth, curved wooden handle.

She was still a block away from the school when she heard the *whoop-whoop*. Now she was going to be late! She had done too much puddle stomping, and not enough straight-ahead walking.

She tried to hurry, but it was difficult to run while carrying her umbrella, especially in her yellow boots.

By the time she reached the outer edges of the school, the eight-minute warning bell was already clanging.

She counted the clangs and was disappointed when they stopped at eight. She was hoping for a porcupine.

Glancing down, she noticed the sidewalk around the school was dry. She stuck out one hand. The rain seemed to have stopped.

She tilted the umbrella a little to the side and looked up.

The Cloud of Doom had kept all the other clouds away, including the rain clouds. Sharie glared at the horrible cloud. It almost seemed alive as it turned and churned inside itself.

Suddenly a gust of wind tore the umbrella from her hand.

Horrified, she watched it bounce across the blacktop toward the school. She chased after it.

The umbrella hit the bike rack and stuck there for a moment. But just as Sharie got there, it swooped upward.

She jumped and managed to grab the curved handle.

The umbrella continued to rise.

She thought about letting go, but she didn't want to lose her umbrella. She held on with both hands.

When she passed the second-floor window, she realized she probably should have let go sooner.

When she rose past the third floor, she wished she had let go at the second floor.

When she reached the fourth floor, she

wished she had let go when she was back at the third floor.

By the time she reached the sixth floor, it was definitely too late.

Her left rain boot slipped off when she passed the ninth floor. She watched it fall the long way down.

Higher and higher, scarier and scarier. She passed the seventeenth floor, the eighteenth, the twentieth.

(There was no nineteenth floor.)

She could see inside the classroom windows as she went past them. Some of the kids waved at her.

She couldn't wave back. She couldn't risk falling.

Although the alternative wasn't much better. If she continued to hang on, she realized, she'd be sucked into the Cloud of Doom.

She passed the twenty-fifth floor, then the twenty-sixth, and the twenty-seventh. She knew the floor numbers by the teachers she saw through the windows.

At the thirtieth floor, she could see her own desk, next to the window.

The window was open.

She closed her eyes, then jumped.

A horn blared.

When Sharie opened her eyes, she lay sprawled across the top of her desk.

"Oh, you *are* here, Sharie," said Mrs. Jewls. "Funny, I didn't see you. I was just about to mark you absent. Were you sleeping?"

Maybe it was a dream. She hoped so. If not, her favorite umbrella was lost forever!

Her left foot felt cold.

On her right foot she wore a yellow rain boot, but on the left, just a thin red sock.

# 14

## MR. K AND DR. P

*(Author's note: Due to strict rules about confidentiality, and to avoid unnecessary embarrassment for those involved, the names of the characters have been omitted from this story. Please don't try to guess.)*

Mr. K headed up the stairs. He wore a paper bag over his head. It was ten o'clock in the morning.

All the little brats—as he liked to call them—should be in class, but he wore the paper bag just in case he encountered a stray one.

When he reached the third floor, he tripped over the top step and fell onto the landing.

"I knew I should have cut out some eyeholes," he said to himself. His knee hurt, but that was the least of his worries. He got back to his feet and limped up the stairs.

Actually, only one eyehole would have helped. His left eye was shut tight. His other eye was wide open. The eyebrow was raised in a constant expression of surprise.

By counting his steps, he knew when he reached the fourth floor. He felt his way to the door, then knocked.

"Yes, who's there?" asked Dr. P from the other side.

Mr. K did not want to say his name aloud in case anyone was listening. He opened the door and entered.

If Dr. P was surprised to see a person with a bag over his head, he didn't show it. He had been trained to keep a straight face, *no matter what*! Whenever someone came to see him, it was part of his job to act like everything was perfectly normal.

"Yes, what seems to be the problem?" he asked, stroking his beard.

Mr. K removed the bag.

"Yikes!" screamed Dr. P, throwing both his hands up in the air.

He quickly regained his composure. "So, why did you come see me?" he asked as he rubbed his beard.

Mr. K made an "uhhhh" noise as he pointed to his face.

"Your face is stuck?" said Dr. P.

Mr. K nodded.

"Please, have a seat."

Mr. K sat on the couch.

Dr. P came closer to get a better look. He poked a puffed-out cheek. "Does this hurt?" he asked.

Mr. K shook his head.

"How about this?" He tugged on the tip of Mr. K's tongue.

Again, Mr. K shook his head.

"Very interesting," said Dr. P.

He walked to the bookshelf. "Hmm . . ." he muttered as he tried to find the book he needed. "This should do it!" he declared, removing a very fat book.

He bonked Mr. K on the top of the head with it.

"Uhh!" exclaimed Mr. K.

"Any better?" Dr. P.

"I bit my tongue," Mr. K said without moving his lips.

"Hmm, this will be more difficult than I thought," said Dr. P. He returned to the bookshelf, chose a different book, and brought it to his desk. He thumbed through the pages. "Cold feet . . . sticky fingers . . . ah, here we are, stuck face!"

He silently read to himself for a minute or two, then looked up and asked, "Did you have a pet when you were a child?"

Mr. K nodded.

Dr. P looked back at his book and read some more.

"A cat?"

Mr. K shook his head.

"A dog?"

He nodded.

"Did you love your dog?"

Mr. K's head didn't move at all. A tear trickled out of his eye and dripped down his face.

"Excellent!" declared Dr. P. "I think we're making real progress."

He shut the book, scooted his chair up close, and leaned toward Mr. K. "Look into my eyes," he said.

With his one eye, Mr. K stared at Dr. P.

Dr. P stared back.

He held up a gold chain with a green stone attached. He let the stone swing gently back and forth between them. Their faces were so close, the stone kept barely missing their noses.

"I'm going to take you back to another time and place," said Dr. P. "You are just a young boy, playing with your dog in your backyard. Your grandmother smiles from the kitchen window. A pie is baking in the oven. You can smell cinnamon."

Mr. K's nose twitched.

"Now your grandmother is outside, holding the pie. She asks if you want some."

Mr. K's tongue remained sticking out. However, it slowly moved from one side of his mouth to the other.

Dr. P noted the breakthrough.

"But instead of giving you a piece of pie," he said, "she smashes it in your face!"

Mr. K's mouth popped open. Then his face snapped back into place.

His eyebrow lowered. His eye opened. His cheek unpuffed. His tongue went back inside where it belonged.

"Why did she do that to me?" he cried.

Dr. P handed him a tissue.

Mr. K wiped his eyes, and then cleaned the imaginary pie off his face. He stood and straightened his suit.

"You won't tell anybody anything about this, will you?" he asked.

"Everything that happens inside this office is strictly confidential," Dr. P assured him.

Mr. K left the office feeling as dignified as ever.

Dr. P leaned back in his chair, with his hands behind his head. He felt very satisfied. It's not every day that he gets to help someone as important as Mr. K.

Dr. P's tongue was sticking out.

His left eyebrow was raised. His right eye was shut tight. And it looked like he was trying to swallow a tennis ball.

# 15

## THE UNBREAKABLES

It's bad enough when two friends fight. It's even worse when three friends pick on a fourth.

Joe and John were best friends.
    "Shut up!" said Joe.
    "You shut up!" said John.

Rondi and Allison were best friends.
    "May I borrow a pencil?" asked Allison.

"Here, stick it up your nose!" said Rondi.

Maybe it was because they were worried and anxious about the Cloud of Doom looming above them. Maybe it was because their fingernails and toenails were growing too fast. For whatever reason, the longer everyone spent beneath the Cloud, the crabbier they got.

Maurecia, Joy, Deedee, and Ron were more than just best friends forever. Their friendship was so strong, they called themselves the "Unbreakables."

Every morning, they met before school by the flagpole. They had a special four-handed handshake. Each would hold out one hand, and they'd lock thumbs to pinkies. Then they'd raise and lower their hands three times and shout, "Unbreakable!"

The lunch bell kaboinked four times, and the Unbreakables headed down the stairs together.

"I wonder what we're having today," Deedee said.

"Didn't you count the kaboinks?" asked Mau-recia.

"Spaghetti and feetballs," said Joy.

"Ooh, I like those," said Deedee.

"You would," said Ron. "They smell as bad as your feet."

He held his nose.

"My feet don't stink," said Deedee.

Joy held her nose too, and said, "Not to you, but to everyone else!"

Maurecia and Ron laughed.

They entered the cafeteria. Deedee took a tray and pushed it to Miss Mush. The lunch teacher handed her a plate of spaghetti topped with a foot-shaped meat patty.

Deedee set the plate on her tray, next to her history book. She was careful not to spill any feetsauce. Her half-finished homework was folded inside the book. It was due after lunch.

She sat down with the others at one of the long tables. She cut off a piece of a feetball, swished it around in the sauce, and ate it.

"You eat the heel first?" asked Maurecia.

"So, what's wrong with that?" asked Deedee.

"It's gross!" said Ron. "You're supposed to start with the toes!"

"Who says?"

"It's just how it's done," said Joy. "Ask anyone."

"You don't know everything!" Deedee said angrily as she shook her fork at her friends.

A bit of sauce dropped on her paper.

"Now look what you did!" she accused them.

"You did it to yourself," said Joy.

Deedee tried to wipe it up with her napkin, but that only made it worse. "Now I have to start all over!" she complained.

Deedee remained in the cafeteria long after her friends left to go play. She still had one question to answer, and one last toe to eat.

It didn't seem fair that her friends were outside playing, while she was stuck inside.

"Stupid Ron," she muttered. "Stupid Maurecia. Stupid Joy. They're the ones with stinky feet!"

When at last she finished, she put her dishes in the dish tray, and dumped her trash. She hurried out of the lunchroom, and down the stairs.

Once outside, she saw them playing

three-square, and wasn't sure if she even wanted to join them.

Suddenly, her face filled with horror. "Oh, no!" she called out, and then pulled her hair with both hands.

She didn't have her homework, or her history book! She turned and ran back into the building.

Miss Mush and Mr. Pepperadder were busy wiping the counter with dishrags when Deedee came rushing up them.

"Hi, Deedee, did you want seconds?" Miss Mush asked hopefully. "We put everything away, but I'd be happy to heat up another plate."

Out of breath, Deedee explained about her book and homework.

Neither Miss Mush nor Mr. Pepperadder remembered seeing it.

"And I've already dumped all the trash," said Mr. Pepperadder.

There were four large dumpsters in the back of Wayside School. A pair of feet was sticking up out of one of them.

Upside down, buried in the trash, Deedee tried to read every wrinkled and soggy piece of paper as she dug through half-eaten feetballs, strands of spaghetti, drippy milk cartons, apple cores, pickle slices, and *who-knows-what-else?*

"It's impossible! There's no way!" she cried.

Then, just when all hope seemed lost, a noise came from somewhere deep inside the dumpster next to hers.

"Found it!" called Ron.

Rustling sounds could be heard from inside the other two dumpsters, as well.

"Hooray!" cheered Maurecia.

"Wow, what a relief!" shouted Joy.

Yes, there were six other feet sticking up from the dumpsters.

They were the Unbreakables. Not even the Cloud of Doom could destroy their friendship.

But that was only the first test. The ultimate test was still to come.

# 16

## A SHORT CHAPTER
## ABOUT A LONG BOOK

*Read a book. Write a book report. Draw a picture.*
That was the assignment Mrs. Jewls put up on
the board.

*(Don't worry. You haven't already read*
*this chapter. Mrs. Jewls assigned lots of*
*book reports. For some reason, she thought*
*reading was important.)*

Whenever Jason looked at the board, he got a heavy feeling in the pit of his stomach—almost as heavy as the 999-page book he lugged around in his backpack. It was like his own Cloud of Doom that he took wherever he went.

He didn't know how he'd ever read it. His book report was already three weeks late.

One time his bookmark fell out. It took him twenty minutes just to find his place.

He was very disappointed to discover he was only on page six.

"Jason, is your book report ready yet?" Mrs. Jewls asked him each day he walked into class.

"Sorry, Mrs. Jewls," he told her. "It's a really, really, really long book."

He always answered the same way, although the number of *really*s varied.

"How do you like your book?" Allison asked him.

"Have you finished it yet?" asked Rondi.

The two girls giggled.

He wondered if anyone had ever read a book with 999 pages. Maybe the author never even finished writing it. Perhaps she quit after 300 pages, figuring nobody would ever get that far anyway.

That evening, however, something strange happened.

Jason was trying to get through page twenty-six, when suddenly he laughed. He read some more, and laughed again.

It was as if he and the character had become friends. He read for an entire hour without realizing it.

When he reached page seventy, something sad happened, and he hoped his sister didn't notice his tears.

He stayed up all night. He read about exciting battles, and strange and goofy animals. No matter how tired he got, he kept needing to know what happened next.

The next day during recess, while everyone else played, Jason preferred to sit by himself with his book. He even liked the kissing parts, but had to keep glancing around, to make sure Allison and Rondi couldn't see what he was reading.

The two girls came toward him.

"He'll never finish it," said Allison.

"No way," Rondi agreed.

"Shh," said Jason. "I'm trying to read."

# 17

## THE BEST PRINCIPAL EVER!!!

Mrs. Jewls went from desk to desk, handing back everyone's history homework. "Nice job, Eric," she said to one of the Erics. "Well done, Eric," she said to another. "You better study the history of cabbage," she told the third Eric. "The Ultimate Test is coming."

The third Eric, naturally, was Eric Ovens. He thought he knew all about the history of cabbage, and felt bad when he saw his home-work grade. Then he realized that Mrs. Jewls had given him Eric Bacon's paper by mistake.

It turned out Eric Bacon had Eric Fry's home-work, and Eric Fry had his.

They switched papers.

Mrs. Jewls moved on. "Nice job, Deedee, although your paper smelled somewhat strange."

She stopped at Jason's desk and shook her head. "I was very disappointed, Jason."

"Sorry," Jason muttered. He could barely hold his head up. "I was up all night reading."

"He'll never finish his book, Mrs. Jewls," said Allison.

Suddenly, the classroom door swung open and banged against the wall. Everyone turned to see Mr. Kidswatter.

"Good morning, children," he said.

They stared at him. He had never been inside their classroom before.

Mr. Kidswatter loudly cleared his throat. "I said, 'Good morning, children . . .'"

Mrs. Jewls hurried to the front of the room.

She waved her hands like an orchestra conductor.

"Good morning, Mr. Kidswatter," the children said in unison.

The principal smiled. "What's all this?" he asked, pointing to the twenty-seven plastic containers stacked against the wall.

"Toenails," said Paul.

"Also fingernails," added Leslie so the principal wouldn't think the class was weird.

"Well, I'm glad to see you're doing important work here," said Mr. Kidswatter.

"Would you like to donate a toenail, or maybe a fingernail?" asked Mrs. Jewls.

Mr. Kidswatter curled his fingers as he examined his nails. "No, I'm still using mine. Anyway, that's not why I'm here. I'm looking for a student to bang the gong on Friday. I figured I'd start at the top, and work my way down, until I found someone willing to—"

Every arm shot up in the air. Calls of "Pick me" and "Ooh, ooh" could be heard from around the room.

"Oh," said Mr. Kidswatter. "I guess it won't take as long as I thought."

"Me, me," begged Bebe, stretching her arm high.

"No, me, me!" urged Deedee.

It was impossible to know where Mr. Kidswatter was looking. He wore mirrored sunglasses, even indoors.

Joy had both hands raised, doubling her chances of being picked. "You're the best principal ever!!!" she called out.

Mr. Kidswatter's head turned. "YOU!!!" he boomed, pointing his finger.

Everybody groaned, except for the one person he had chosen.

"Me?" Stephen asked meekly.

"You?" asked Mr. Kidswatter, sounding somewhat surprised. "Yes, you!" he declared. "I chose you, didn't I? And I don't make mistakes!"

He strode toward Stephen, then placed his big hands on both sides of Stephen's desk and leaned over. "Be in my office on Friday, at two minutes before three o'clock!" he ordered. "You will get one, and only one, swing of the mallet, so you better not miss! You must hit the very center of the gong, at exactly three o'clock. Not a second early! Not a second late!! There are no second chances!!!"

Stephen's right leg was shaking.

The principal straightened up and headed toward the door. "Good-bye, children," he said.

He stopped.

He waited.

He folded his arms across his chest.

Mrs. Jewls waved her arms like an orchestra conductor.

"Good-bye, Mr. Kidswatter," everyone said together.

As soon as the principal was gone, everyone crowded around Stephen's desk.

"You are so lucky!" said Jason.

"This is the best thing that has ever happened to anyone in our class!" said Jenny.

"You better not blow it!" said Joy. "Or else no kid will ever get to ring the gong again!"

"Can you even lift the mallet?" asked Terrence.

Stephen didn't say anything. He hadn't heard a word they said.

It was as if the moment Mr. Kidswatter had said, "YOU!!!" someone had banged a gong inside Stephen's head.

*GONNN-nnnn-NNNNN-nnnnn-NNN-NN-nnnnn-NNNNNGGGG!!!*

# 18

# THE MIRROR

Dr. Pickle kept two things on his desk. One was a bust of Sigmund Freud.

A *bust* is a statue of someone's head, neck, and shoulders. Sigmund Freud was the most famous psychologist ever. He was Dr. Pickle's hero.

Dr. Freud also had a beard.

The second thing on Dr. Pickle's desk was a handheld mirror. Dr. Pickle checked his beard at least five times per day, to make sure it was trimmed just right.

Now, however, that was the least of his worries. He looked at his face in the mirror. His cheek was puffed out. His tongue was sticking out. One eye was closed. One eyebrow was raised.

He looked like a big doofus!

He gently swung his pickle stone between his face and the mirror.

"I am getting sleepy," he said to himself. "By the count of five, I will fall asleep. One . . . two . . . thruppledub." His head plopped down on his desk.

This would normally be the time when Dr. Pickle would tell his patient what she was supposed to do when she woke up. But he was his own patient. And both patient and doctor were sleeping.

Sometime later, a car horn blared. It sounded like there was an angry driver right behind him.

Dr. Pickle woke up. He had no idea how long he'd been sleeping. It took him a moment to remember who he was, where he was, and why he had tried to hypnotize himself.

He picked up the mirror and checked his face. No change.

"Now what am I going to do?" he asked.

That was strange.

He had felt his mouth move when he spoke, but the mouth in the mirror didn't move.

He brought his hands to his face. He could see his hands touching the face in the mirror too.

The cheek in the mirror was still all puffed out, but his own cheek felt soft and flat. He moved his tongue around inside his mouth, even though the tongue in the mirror was sticking out at him.

He set the mirror on his desk.

"This is very interesting," he said aloud. Clearly, the face shifts to whoever stares at it, he realized.

He turned the mirror over, facedown.

He hadn't read about this in any of his psychiatry books. He slowly raised the mirror, caught a glimpse of the hideous face that was still there, then quickly lowered it back down on his desk.

This discovery would make him famous! He picked up the bust of Sigmund Freud. "Even more famous than you," he said to it.

But would all that fame be worth it? What if someone else's face got stuck along the way?

"What would you do?" he asked Dr. Freud.

There is a reason it is called a bust. It was made of bronze, and felt heavy in his hand.

He flipped the mirror over, and slammed Sigmund Freud down on top of it.

The face shattered.

Up in Mrs. Jewls's class, Kathy suddenly felt very dizzy and confused.

She looked at the sentence she had just written. "I can't read this!" she exclaimed. "It's backward."

"Let me see," said D.J., taking it from her. "How did you do that? That is so cool!"

"Warm!" Kathy replied.

# 19

## PUSH-DOWNS

Stephen lay on the playground, surrounded by his classmates. He grunted as he pushed down on the blacktop with all his might.

Nothing happened.

"You can do it!" urged Maurecia.

"Push harder, Stephen!" encouraged Joe.

Stephen pushed harder. He grunted louder.

Still, nothing.

Louis, the yard teacher, blew his whistle.

"What's going on here?" he asked as he made his way to Stephen.

"Stephen is trying to do a push-down," said Dameon.

"You mean a push-up," corrected Kathy.

"Why do you have to be so opposite all the time?" asked Dameon. "Stephen isn't pushing *up*. He's pushing *down*!"

"So he can go up," said Myron.

Kathy didn't mean to be opposite. She'd discovered she liked being nice and having friends. She just really thought they were called *push-ups*.

"How many has he done so far?" asked Louis.

"None," said Jason. "But he's trying really hard."

Louis kneeled and then patted Stephen on the back. "Keep at it, Stephen," he encouraged. "Every day you'll get a little stronger. In a month, I bet you'll be able to do five push-downs."

"A month!" exclaimed Deedee. "Stephen doesn't have a month."

"He has to bang the gong on Friday!" explained Ron.

Louis raised one eyebrow. His mustache

twitched. "I guess he really is the best principal ever!!!" he muttered.

"What?" asked Mac.

"Never mind," said Louis. "Push hard, Stephen. The mallet is made of solid iron."

Stephen grunted louder than ever. He didn't move. "I can't do it, Louis," he gasped. "Talk to Mr. Kidswatter. Tell him to pick somebody else!"

"Ooh, me!" exclaimed Joy.

"Mr. Kidswatter is the smartest principal in the school," said Louis. "He must have had a very good reason for choosing you."

@. @. @.

"Would you like to donate a toenail, or maybe a fingernail?" Mrs. Jewls asked.

Mr. Kidswatter examined his nails. "No, I'm still using mine. I need a student to bang the gong on Friday."

The next thing he knew all the little brats had their arms in the air, and they were making strange noises, like "Ooh, ooh!" and "Me, me!"

"You're the best principal ever!!!" someone shouted.

Those were magic words. He turned to see who had shouted them, when suddenly he saw HER—that awful girl who had given him that awful face.

"YOU!!!" he boomed, pointing at Dana.

Dana had a mosquito bite on her ankle, however, and at that moment, she bent down to scratch it.

Stephen sat behind Dana.

⊚ ⊚ ⊚

He lay on the blacktop, staring up at the awful Cloud. "I'm doomed," he moaned.

"Look, Stephen, I don't know what will happen on Friday," Louis admitted. "I don't know if you'll hit the gong, or drop the mallet on your toe. But I know this. You have to try. Or else you will regret it every day for the rest of your life. And whenever you hear a gong, your heart will fill with a terrible sadness."

"You really don't hear gongs all that often," Myron pointed out. "I mean, except here."

"Even if you make a million dollars someday," Louis continued. "You could buy your own gong, and hit it every day, all alone in your great big mansion. But it won't be the same."

"That is so sad," said Leslie.

Paul sniffed back a tear.

"So, what do you say, Stephen?" asked Louis. "You want to give it one more try?"

Stephen wished Louis hadn't mentioned dropping the mallet on his toe. Now that was all he could think about.

He sighed, and then rolled back over. He pushed as hard as he could.

"You can do it, Stephen!" urged Allison.

"Push!" said Jason.

"Up!" encouraged Kathy. "I mean down. I mean up. I mean . . ."

Now she was really confused.

Stephen rose an inch off the ground, then collapsed.

Everyone cheered.

"One more," urged Louis. "And then we'll go to the monkey bars and do some pull-downs."

# 20

## INSIDE THE CLOSET

Jason did it! He finished reading all 999 pages.

He was so tired, he didn't know how he made it up the stairs to Mrs. Jewls's class. He fell asleep somewhere around the fourth floor and awoke on the twenty-eighth.

"Did you finish your book, yet?" Allison asked him when he entered the classroom.

She and Rondi giggled.

"Yep," said Jason.

The girls' mouths dropped open.

His book report only had to be one page, but Jason had written ten pages. It was impossible to write only one page about a 999-page book.

He wondered if anybody had ever written a book with more pages. Probably not. There was probably a law against writing a book with a thousand pages or more.

He brought the ten pages, and his three pictures, to Mrs. Jewls's desk. "I guess if somebody writes a book with nine hundred and ninety-nine pages, it has to be really good," he said. "Or else nobody would ever read it."

"I don't know," Mrs. Jewls admitted. "I've never read a book that long."

Jason sleepily handed over all his papers.

"Where's your paper clip?" asked Mrs. Jewls.

"It got all bent in my backpack," he explained, too tired to think about what he was saying. "Unbent really. I guess the nine-hundred-and-ninety-nine-page book was too heavy for it."

He showed Mrs. Jewls his paper clip, now

unbent into a crooked line.

Mrs. Jewls put her hand to her mouth, horrified. "You bent your paper clip?" she gasped.

"Unbent," said Jason.

Mrs. Jewls stood up. "You better come with me!" she exclaimed. She grabbed Jason by his ear and yanked him toward the door.

"Ow," he whimpered.

Whispers could be heard from all around the room.

"*He read a nine-hundred-and-ninety-nine-page book!*"

"*But he bent his paper clip.*"

"*He wrote a ten-page book report.*"

"*But he bent his paper clip.*"

"*No, he unbent it.*"

"Everyone stop talking, now!" ordered Mrs. Jewls. "Do not leave your seats for any reason!" She pulled Jason out of the room and slammed the classroom door behind her.

She dragged him straight to the closet that wasn't there.

Jason read the signs. *"KEEP BACK!" "DO NOT*

OPEN DOORS!" "DANGER!" "CALL THE FIRE DEPARTMENT IF YOU SMELL SOMETHING UNUSUAL!"

He sniffed.

He didn't smell anything.

Yet.

Mrs. Jewls turned the dial on the padlock as she quietly said the combination to herself. "Twenty-four . . . seventeen . . . six."

The lock opened.

"But you said it wasn't there," Jason pointed out.

"Of course it's there," said Mrs. Jewls. "Hold this." She gave Jason one end of the heavy chain.

He remained where he was as Mrs. Jewls took the other end and walked four times around the closet, unwrapping it. Then she took Jason's end from him and tossed the chain aside.

It clanged against the floor.

A steel bar, held in place by two clamps, still blocked the closet doors. The locks on the clamps had letters instead of numbers.

Jason watched as Mrs. Jewls set one lock to

ACBD and the other lock to BDBC.

The clamps snapped open.

"I'm really sorry about the paper clip, Mrs. Jewls," said Jason.

"It's a little late for that now, don't you think?" said his teacher. She lifted the steel bar and tossed it aside. A loud *CLANK* echoed down and up the stairs.

Mrs. Jewls walked down several steps. Jason watched, amazed, as she slid open a secret compartment hidden in the third step from the top.

She removed two keys, one red and one green.

Each closet door had a keyhole; one was green, the other red. Mrs. Jewls put the green key in the red hole, and the red key in the green hole.

"I have to turn them toward each other, at precisely the same time," she said, "or else it will trigger the sirens and smoke screen."

Jason held his breath as he watched her turn the keys.

The doors clicked open.

Ever since the closet first appeared, he and his friends had been trying to guess what was inside it. They imagined all kinds of horrible things, but what Jason saw now was worse than anything they ever imagined.

The closet was empty.

"Don't lock me in there, Mrs. Jewls!" he pleaded. "I didn't do it on purpose. The book was too heavy!"

He tried to remember all that he had seen and heard. *Third step from the top. Red key in green hole. 27-6-14. ABDC.*

It was too much! It was slipping out of his brain faster than he could remember.

*"CALL THE FIRE DEPARTMENT IF YOU SMELL SOMETHING UNUSUAL!"*

"I don't want to become an unusual smell!" he cried.

"What are you blabbering about?" asked Mrs. Jewls. "Why would I lock you in the closet?"

She bent over.

Jason looked again. The closet wasn't completely empty, after all. There, in the back corner, was a small cardboard box.

Mrs. Jewls picked it up. A price tag stuck to its side read, "89¢."

Mrs. Jewls opened the top flap and removed a paper clip.

"Now, don't tell anyone where you got this," she said as she handed it to him.

"I won't," he promised.

She put the box back in the closet, then shut and locked the doors, turning the color-coded keys in opposite directions. She returned the keys to their secret hiding place.

She grunted as she lifted the steel bar, and then again when she set it in place. She snapped the clamps shut and spun the dials on the locks.

Jason picked up one end of the chain and walked four times around the closet. Mrs. Jewls secured the padlock.

"I'm very proud of you, Jason, for finishing the whole book," she said.

"I was kind of sorry when it ended," said Jason.

Teacher and student returned to class.

# 21

## BREATHE

Stephen stared at the clock on the wall.

What if he couldn't lift the mallet? What if he dropped it on his toe? What if he dropped it on Mr. Kidswatter's toe? He could be expelled!

"Breathe," said Jason from the desk next to him.

Stephen took a breath.

He stared at the clock.

What if someone left a skateboard on the stairs? Then he might trip over it on his way to the gong. If he broke his leg, Mr. Kidswatter would yell at him for being late!

"Breathe," said Rondi from the desk on his other side.

Stephen took a breath.

He stared at the clock. Sometimes, it seemed the hands didn't move at all. Other times, he'd blink, and it would be half an hour later.

Time didn't always make sense at Wayside School.

For lunch, Miss Mush made pepper-only pizza. Stephen ate his slice, but did not remember eating it. His only clue was that he was very thirsty and his tongue and lips burned.

He returned to his seat in Mrs. Jewls's class. He stared at the clock.

Jenny was late coming back from lunch. "Sorry, Mrs. Jewls," she said. "I can't find my skateboard."

"Oh, no!" Stephen shouted.

"Are you all right, Stephen?" Mrs. Jewls asked him.

"Why did he have to pick me?" Stephen moaned.

"If you didn't want to do it, why'd you raise your hand?" asked Mac.

"Everyone else had their hands raised," Stephen explained. "I mean, I guess I was excited about it at the time, but now . . ."

"You have cold feet," said Mrs. Jewls.

"Yes!" exclaimed Stephen. He wondered how Mrs. Jewls knew that. His feet felt like two blocks of ice. No wonder she was a teacher! But what did his frozen feet have to do with ringing the gong?

"Breathe," said Mrs. Jewls.

Stephen took a breath.

Mrs. Jewls's class always had music on Friday afternoons. "I'm sorry, we don't have musical instruments today," she announced. "They were sent out to be cleaned, and we haven't gotten them back yet."

What if the gong was being washed too? Would he have to bang it on a different day?

"Breathe," said Kathy.

Stephen took a breath.

"So just use what you were born with!" said Mrs. Jewls. "And a one, and a two . . ."

Dana loudly blew her nose. Ron twiddled his lips. Mac puffed out his cheek and popped it with a flick of a finger. Calvin and Bebe whistled. Joe stood on his head and sang "Jingle Bells."

Paul pulled Leslie's pigtails. She shrieked, squealed, or squawked, depending on the pull.

"Stop the music!" Mrs. Jewls suddenly shouted, and the room became instantly quiet.

"Stephen, you're late," she told him. "I'm sorry. I was so carried away by the music, I didn't notice the time."

"Time?" said Stephen.

"Now, Stephen!" said Mrs. Jewls.

He remained frozen in his chair.

Mrs. Jewls asked Jason and Rondi to help.

They moved to either side of Stephen and slowly lifted him to a standing position. "It's time, buddy," said Jason.

"Time," Stephen repeated.

He took one step, then stopped.

"Now the other leg," said Rondi.

He took another step.

"You can do it, Stephen!" cheered Kathy.

"Bang that gong like no one ever banged it before!" called Joy.

Stephen walked across the room. He stepped out the door. Behind him, he heard the entire class shout together.

"Breathe!"

Stephen took a breath.

# 22

## THE MOMENT

Stephen was worrying his way down the stairs when suddenly he spotted Jenny's skateboard, right in the middle of a step. He stepped over it.

Well, that was easy.

And just like that, his fears vanished. Not even the Cloud of Doom worried him.

He quickly hurried the rest of the way down. He didn't want to be late. When he reached the second floor, he could see Louis below, wheeling the gong into place.

"Louis!" he shouted, and then jumped down the final eight steps. "Am I late?"

"You're right on time," said the yard teacher.

The gong was gigantic, almost twice as big as Stephen. He had never stood so close to it before. In the center was a small red dot.

The iron mallet hung from a hook. The mallet was longer than his arm, and thicker too.

"Have you been doing your push-downs?" Louis asked.

Stephen nodded. "I'm almost up to two," he said confidently.

Mr. Kidswatter stepped out of his office. He took one look at Stephen and asked, "Who are you?"

"This is Stephen," said Louis. "You chose him to bang the gong today?"

"Him? Why would I choose him?"

"Because you're the best principal ever!!!" said Louis.

"Well, yes, that's true," said Mr. Kidswatter.

"I'll do my best, sir," said Stephen.

"That's what worries me," said the principal.

Louis handed Stephen two cotton balls.

As Stephen was stuffing them in his ears, Louis unhooked the mallet.

He held it out to Stephen.

Stephen wobbled as he took the mallet with both hands. Louis helped him raise it to his shoulder.

Mr. Kidswatter checked his watch, and then started the countdown.

"Ten! Nine! Eight!"

He had to shout the numbers, so Stephen could hear him through the cotton balls.

"Seven! Six!"

Stephen tightened his grip on the handle.

"Five! Four!"

Stephen groaned loudly as he slowly raised the iron mallet up off his shoulder. It was a good thing he'd been doing all those push-downs.

"Three!"

Stephen staggered, but maintained his balance.

"Two!"

He concentrated on the red dot.

"One!!!"

He swung with all his might . . . and missed!

He didn't just miss the red dot. He missed the gong.

Louis jumped out of the way as the weight of the mallet pulled Stephen around in a circle.

The second time around, the mallet banged into the gong, right on the dot.

*GONNNNNN–nnnnnn–NNNNNN–nnnnnn–NNNNNN–nnnnnn . . .*

Despite the cotton balls, the sound echoed inside Stephen's skull, and rattled his bones.

*. . . NNNNNN–nnnnnn–NNNNNN–nnnnnn–NNNNNNN–*

It traveled up the stairs, all the way to the thirtieth floor.

*. . . nnnnnn-NNNNNNG!*

"He did it!" shouted Mac.

"Yay, Stephen!" yelled Jenny.

Everyone in Mrs. Jewls's class whooped and hollered.

Louis kept Stephen from falling over, and

took the mallet from him. He hooked it to the frame, and then he and Stephen wheeled the gong into the principal's office.

Mr. Kidswatter was already there, standing by the door. The principal held out his big hand and said, "Well done, Stephen!"

In the history of Wayside School, Stephen was the only kid to ever shake Mr. Kidswatter's hand.

In the future, whenever Stephen feels worried, or frustrated, or just plain sad, his mind will take him back to the moment the mallet struck the gong. He will close his eyes and see the red dot. His hands will feel the weight of the iron mallet. He will hear the sound of the gong bouncing back and forth between his ears, and will feel the vibrations in his bones.

And he will smile.

# 23

# BLAME IT ON THE CLOUD

Mrs. Jewls went from desk to desk as she handed back the arithmetic test. "I'm very disappointed in you, Joy," she said. "You need to learn your sixes and sevens."

Joy had gotten an F. That awful letter was written in red ink, and there was a circle around it.

"But it wasn't my fault, Mrs. Jewls," Joy

complained. "It's the Cloud of Doom. It made me change my answers!"

"Hmmm," said Mrs. Jewls as she took another look at Joy's test. She made two little strokes with her red pen, changing the F to a B.

Joy smiled.

The door swung open and Bebe walked in more than fifteen minutes late.

"Bebe, you need to put your name on the board under DISCIPLINE," Mrs. Jewls told her.

"Don't blame me," said Bebe. "I left my house on time. The Cloud of Doom slowed me down."

"Oh. Okay, then," said Mrs. Jewls.

Leslie screamed.

Mrs. Jewls turned.

"Paul pulled my pigtails!" she accused. "Both at the same time!"

"Paul, what do you have to say for yourself?" demanded Mrs. Jewls.

Paul shrugged. "Cloud-a-Doom?" he tried.

Leslie turned around and shook her fist at Paul. "I'll doom you, you ugly bug sniffer!"

"Leslie, that's no way to talk!" said Mrs. Jewls.

"It wasn't me, Mrs. Jewls," Leslie said sweetly. "The Cloud of Doom made me say it."

"Well, apologize to Paul for calling him ugly."

"But I didn't call him ugly," said Leslie. "He sniffs ugly bugs."

Jenny and D.J. laughed. Mrs. Jewls glared at them.

"Cloud-a-Doom," they said at the same time.

Mrs. Jewls continued to hand back the tests. "You can do better, Terrence," she said, when she came to him.

Terrence crumpled his test into a ball and brought it to the front of the room, where he dropped it in the trash. He stood there a moment, staring at the trash basket.

"Terrence, return to your seat!" ordered Mrs. Jewls.

He stayed where he was.

"Terrence, do you have a problem?" asked Mrs. Jewls.

"No," said Terrence. "No problem." He kicked the basket. It sailed end over end across the classroom, spilling trash along the way.

Mac raised both arms like a football ref.

"Three points!" he declared.

"Terrence!" exclaimed Mrs. Jewls.

"Sorry, the Cloud of Doom made me do it," said Terrence.

"Mac," said Mrs. Jewls. "You know better."

"Cloud of—"

"Enough!" shouted Mrs. Jewls. "I get it. It's hard with that cloud hanging over us all the time. But you can't blame it for everything that goes wrong. You have to take responsibility. And that means working extra hard so things don't go wrong! So, I'm doubling all your homework."

"That's not fair!" complained Benjamin.

Mrs. Jewls told Benjamin to write his name on the blackboard under the word DISCIPLINE.

"The Ultimate Test will start Monday," Mrs. Jewls declared. "It will take three days to complete, and you better be prepared, cloud or no cloud!"

There were lots of groans.

Mrs. Jewls returned to Joy's desk. She crossed out the B, and this time gave her an F minus.

"Terrence, there's a broom in the back closet. I want you to pick up the trash basket and sweep the floor. Mac will help you.

"Everyone else, get in line behind Benjamin, and write your names on the blackboard under DISCIPLINE."

There were more moans and groans as everyone rose from their seats.

"Except you, Todd," ordered Mrs. Jewls. "You're the only one who's been good."

Todd sat back down. He scratched his head.

"You used to be a nice teacher," said Rondi as she made her way to the blackboard.

"Why are you so mean?" asked Allison.

Mrs. Jewls just shrugged, and said, "Cloud-a-Doom."

Above them, the dark cloud continued to churn, as it turned itself inside out again and again. No one hardly noticed it anymore, but it continued to grow larger and more powerful every day.

Lightning flashed inside the cloud, where no one could see it. Thunder boomed where no one could hear it. What happened in the cloud, stayed in the cloud.

For now.

# 24

## THE ULTIMATE TEST,
## DAY ONE

The four Unbreakables met by the flagpole before school. "Don't worry, Maurecia," said Joy. "When you get sent back to kindergarten, I will still be your friend."

"Thanks," said Maurecia. "I know you'll do great. Nobody can jump rope like you can."

"True," Joy agreed.

"And Ron's memorized every page in the dictionary," said Deedee.

Ron smiled. "Joy's a good speller too," he pointed out. "You always get a hundred percent on your spelling tests."

"True," Joy agreed.

"And one of Deedee's legs is shorter than the other," said Maurecia.

Deedee smiled. "Just lucky I guess," she admitted.

They locked thumbs and pinkies and shouted, "Unbreakable!"

Maurecia glanced up at the Cloud of Doom, then followed her friends into the school building.


"I hope everyone's ready," Mrs. Jewls greeted her class. "You just need to remember everything you've ever learned in your whole life."

The children looked nervously around.

The test would last three days. Each day would have several minor tests, and one Major Event. On day one, the Major Event was a spelling bee.

"You mean we have to spell the words *out loud*?" asked Joy.

"That's how a spelling bee works," said Mrs. Jewls.

Joy did a lot better when she could write the words. She was a master of fudge-squiggles. If she didn't know the letter, she made a fudge-squiggle that could have been any number of letters. Mrs. Jewls always gave her the benefit of the doubt.

All the children stood along the wall as they waited for their turns. If they missed a word, they would have to sit down.

Mac couldn't spell *curious*. Leslie missed *squawked*. Jason went out on *confidential*.

"Dilly-dally," said Mrs. Jewls.

"Dilly-dally," Todd repeated. He got every letter right, but left out the hyphen.

"It's not even a letter," he protested, when Mrs. Jewls told him to sit down.

Jenny missed *skateboard*.

Joy was next.

"Helicopter," said Mrs. Jewls.

"Helicopter," Joy repeated. "H-e-l—" She was stuck. She didn't know if there was one or two l's, and she didn't know if the letter after that was an e or an i. If she could have written it, she could have made the perfect fudge-squiggles to cover all the possibilities.

She returned to her seat.

Deedee was eliminated on *eliminated*. A short leg didn't help with spelling.

After a while, only three students remained: John, Ron, and Maurecia.

"Spectacle," said Mrs. Jewls.

"Spectacle," John repeated. "S-k-e-p-t-i-c-a-l."

Only Ron and Maurecia remained.

"Orchestra," said Mrs. Jewls.

Murmurs could be heard around the room. Nobody thought Ron could do it.

"Orchestra," Ron repeated, and then spelled it perfectly.

"Vacuum," said Mrs. Jewls.

Maurecia wasn't sure if there were two c's and one u, or two u's and one c, but she guessed right.

Mrs. Jewls closed her dictionary. "Well, that's all the dictionary words," she announced. "I guess I'll have to use words that aren't in the dictionary."

It was Ron's turn.

"Thruppledub," said Mrs. Jewls.

Ron had memorized the entire dictionary. How was he supposed to spell un-dictionary words? "May I have the definition?" he asked.

"It's when you count to three, and fall asleep in the middle," said Mrs. Jewls.

"Oh, that's easy," Ron said, then correctly spelled the nonword.

"Fudge-squiggle," said Mrs. Jewls.

Maurecia spelled it perfectly. She even included the hyphen, having learned from Todd's earlier mistake.

"Whummph," said Mrs. Jewls.

Again Ron asked for the definition.

"It's the sound made by a jump rope as it brushes against the ground," explained Mrs. Jewls.

Ron gave it his best shot. "W-h-u-m-p-h."

"I'm sorry, Ron," said Mrs. Jewls. "There are two m's in whummph."

"I win!" Maurecia exclaimed.

The class cheered.

Ron felt cheated. If it's a made-up word, who gets to decide the number of m's?

Maurecia's smile was big and bright.

Ron was not smiling.

# 25

## JUMP ROPE ARITHMETIC

On day two, the Major Event was Jump Rope Arithmetic. It is just what you'd expect from the name. The children had to answer arithmetic problems while jumping rope.

They earned one point for each jump of a rope. They could choose either to use one rope, or two at a time. Two ropes were harder, but the points added up more quickly.

If they answered a problem wrong, or tripped

over a rope, they were done.

Joy, of course, chose two ropes. This was her special talent, like Joe's upside-down "Jingle Bells," or Dana's funny faces.

"Four plus seven?" asked Mrs. Jewls.

*Whummph.* "Eleven," replied Joy. *Whummph.*

Two points, and she'd only had to answer one question.

*Whummph.* "Three times nine?" *Whummph.*

"Twenty"—*whummph*—"seven." *Whummph.*

She continued with ease, skipping lightly over the ropes while rattling off answers. Louis and Miss Nogard turned the ropes for her.

Miss Nogard was everyone's favorite substitute teacher, especially Louis's.

By the time Joy reached sixty-five points, nearly everybody else in her class had finished jumping.

Ron had earned twenty-three points.

Deedee only got to six. Jumping rope wasn't easy for her, since one leg was shorter than the other.

D.J. had the highest score so far, with eighty-four points.

In the history of the Ultimate Test, nobody had ever broken a hundred.

*Whummph-whummph.*

"Twelve divided by four?" asked Mrs. Jewls.

*Whummph-whummph.* "Three," said Joy. *Whummph-whummph.*

A circle of children had formed around her. They cheered each correct answer.

"Go, Joy, go!" shouted Mac.

When she reached eighty points, even Mrs. Jewls started to get excited.

"Thirty-eight"—*whummph*—"plus fourteen?" *Whummph.*

"Fifty-two!" *Whummph-whummph.*

She was now tied with D.J.!

"One hundred and"—*whummph*—"forty-three"—*whummph*—"divided by" —*whummph*— "eleven?"

"Thirteen!"

Everyone took up Mac's call. "Go, Joy, go! Go, Joy, go!" they chanted.

Louis's and Miss Nogard's arms were getting tired, but they continued to twirl the ropes. They knew they were a part of history.

Joy was now up to ninety-nine!

"Go, Joy, go! Go, Joy, go!"

*Whummph-whummph.* "Twenty-nine times four?" shouted Mrs. Jewls.

*Whummph-whummph.* "One hundred and sixteen," Joy easily answered.

Everyone whooped and hollered. "That's a new world record!" exclaimed Deedee.

*Whummph-whummph.* "Six times seven?"

*Whummphraaaapp!*

Joy lay sprawled across the blacktop. Sixes and sevens always tripped her up.

Still, she had broken one hundred, and set a new world record!

Her classmates rushed up to her.

"You're the best ever!" said Kathy.

"True," Joy agreed.

There was one jumper left.

*Whummph.*

"Sixteen minus eleven?"

*Whummph.*

"Five," said Maurecia.

Maurecia used only one rope. Miss Mush and Mr. Pepperadder turned it for her.

She jumped with both feet at the same time, and held her breath every time she jumped.

*Whummph.*

"Nine times eight?"

*Whummph.*

"Seventy-two."

*Whummph.*

Joy continued to lie on the blacktop as she listened to the slow whummphing. She imagined the solid gold trophy with her name on it. Her picture would be in newspapers all around the world. She'd go on TV, where famous people would ask her questions about jumping rope and arithmetic. Maybe they'd put her in a movie.

When she came out of her daydream, she was surprised to hear the jump rope still whummphing.

"Zero times a thousand."

*Whummph.*

"Zero."

Joy sat up to see that a circle of kids had sur-rounded Maurecia. They cheered every one of her answers.

*Whummph.*

She headed over and poked Todd in the back of his neck. "What's her score so far?"

"Sixty-six," he told her.

Joy wasn't too worried. She was sure her best friend would whummphraaaappp at any moment.

She didn't start to worry until Maurecia reached eighty.

*Whummph.*

"Sixteen times seventeen."

*Whummph.*

"Two hundred and seventy-two."

*Whummph.*

*Well, sure,* Joy thought bitterly. Sixteens and seventeens were a lot easier than sixes and sevens.

🍎 🍎 🍎

In the end, Maurecia whummphraaaapped on an easy one, two plus three.

She was probably just tired. She had been jumping for almost an hour and had earned 211 points.

Joy didn't see her fall. She had quit watching long before.

# 26

## THE ULTIMATE, ULTIMATE TEST

Yes, that's two *ultimate*s.

The word *ultimate* has two meanings. It could mean *final*, or it could mean *most important*.

The Stairway Quiz was both. It was the final event of the third day, and it counted double.

The students were worn out before they started. They'd already had the science crawl, right and left handwriting, animal imitations, upside-down singing, and blindfolded smelling.

The Stairway Quiz would require knowledge, stamina, and most important, speed.

This was Deedee's special talent.

Deedee was a pretty fast runner on flat ground, but she was even faster going up and down stairs. That was because her left leg was a little bit shorter than her right leg. Or maybe it was the other way around. Either way, it gave her an obvious advantage.

Louis, the yard teacher, stood next to the bottom step. "On your mark!" he called out. "Get set!"

Louis blew his whistle.

The children rushed past him, knees pumping and elbows flailing.

Deedee started way back in the pack, but besides her uneven legs, she had another advantage. She was skinny and short. She could squeeze past the slower kids ahead of her.

And they were all slower than Deedee.

As she neared the third floor, only Dameon remained ahead of her.

A man with a black mustache was waiting on the landing.

"How many quarts in a gallon?" he asked Dameon.

"Eight," said Dameon.

Dameon was sent back down to the first floor.

"Name a city in England," he said to Deedee.

"London!" Deedee shouted, then continued on up.

Dr. Pickle was waiting on the fourth floor. "Are dreams real?" he asked.

Deedee was stumped. She could hear other kids charging up the stairs behind her. She hated to have to go back down.

"They're real dreams," she said.

Dr. Pickle rubbed his beard. "Very interesting answer," he said, and let her pass.

By the time she reached the ninth floor, she could only hear distant footsteps behind her.

"What do you call someone who writes books?" asked Mrs. Surlaw.

"You don't *call* them," said Deedee. "You

must never interrupt a great author during her moment of inspiration."

"I think you said the correct answer in there somewhere," the librarian decided.

On the twelfth floor, the man with the mustache was waiting again. Deedee wondered how he had gotten ahead of her.

"Name the largest river in the United States."

Deedee couldn't remember its name, but she knew how to spell it. "M-i-s-s-i-s-s-i-p-p-i!"

Miss Mush asked the question on the fifteenth floor. "How many points on a fork?"

Deedee formed a picture of a fork in her mind, but when she tried to count the points, they blurred.

"Three?" she tried.

"I'm so sorry, Deedee," said Miss Mush.

She didn't have to go all the way back down to the bottom, just to the tenth.

Ron was coming up the other way. "Hi, Deedee," he greeted her.

"Hi, Ron," said Deedee. "Hope you studied your forks and spoons?"

She reached the tenth, answered another question there, then again on the eleventh and twelfth.

Ron was coming down.

"Hi, Ron."

"Hi, Deedee."

She reached Miss Mush a second time.

"What was Christopher Columbus's favorite vegetable?" asked the lunch lady.

Deedee knew that one. "Cabbage!"

She had spent two whole nights studying the history of cabbage.

When she reached the eighteenth floor, the man with the mustache was there again.

"Are zebras black with white stripes, or white with black stripes?"

Deedee thought it was the same thing, but knew that had to be wrong. "The first one," she guessed.

"Was that white with black stripes, or black with white stripes?"

"I don't remember," said Deedee.

"Me neither," the man admitted, and let her pass.

A tall, thin woman asked the next question. She looked like a teacher, but Deedee had never seen her before. Strangely, the woman had one very long fingernail on her pinky.

"Please recite the alphabet backward."

Deedee had to close her eyes to concentrate. "Z, Y, X . . ."

It took her a long time. In her mind, Deedee had to keep saying the alphabet forward, in order to figure out the next backward letter.

She could hear footsteps coming closer, and then Maurecia came up alongside her.

"What are you stopping for?" Maurecia asked.

Deedee looked around. The woman with the long fingernail was gone. "C, B A!" she finished, just in case.

Deedee and Maurecia continued up together, reaching the twentieth floor at the same time. The mustache man was back again.

"How many toes does a three-toed sloth have?" he asked.

That had to be the easiest question yet, thought Deedee. "Three," she said.

"Twelve," said Maurecia.

Deedee was sent back down to the fifteenth floor.

Now she really had to turn on the jets. She leaped around and over the other kids on her way down, and then, using her uneven legs, she practically flew back up the stairs, as she answered all the questions correctly.

She shot past Maurecia between the twenty-eighth and twenty-ninth floors, answered a question about the different kinds of dirt, and then finally reached the top of the stairs where Mrs. Jewls was waiting.

"How many points on a fork?" Mrs. Jewls asked.

"I already had that question," Deedee said as she took several long deep breaths. Her heart was pounding.

"Good, then you know the answer."

Once again, Deedee tried to picture a fork in her mind. It was either three or four.

"Twelve!" she declared, still confused about the sloth, with its three toes and four feet.

She trudged back down.

"Hi, Deedee," said Maurecia on her way up.

Deedee didn't say hi back.

After school, only three of the Unbreakables could be seen by the flagpole.

Maurecia was still inside the school. Photographers were snapping her picture, and she was being questioned by newspaper reporters from all around the world.

When she finally came outside, she was carrying a giant trophy.

"Sorry I took so long," she said.

"You must think you're really great," said Joy.

Maurecia shrugged.

"Well, you should!" said Ron.

"Because you are!" said Deedee.

Maurecia set down her trophy and said, "You guys are the greatest friends ever!"

They held out their hands, locked pinkies and thumbs, and shouted, "Unbreakable!"

Friends stick by each other when one is down. That is a true test of friendship.

But sometimes, it is harder to stick by a friend who is up.

That is the ultimate test of friendship.

$$\begin{array}{r} 999{,}962 \\ +\phantom{99}37 \\ \hline 9 \end{array}$$

# 27

## KACHOOGA BOOP

The Ultimate Test was over, and nobody was sent back to kindergarten. Mrs. Jewls had made up the test so that every one of her students had a chance to shine, using his or her special talent.

"Anyone with nail clippings?" she asked.

Myron came to the front of the room and dropped thirty-seven clippings into the nail bucket. Nineteen came from toes, and eighteen from fingers. He started to do the math on the board.

$$
\begin{array}{r}
999{,}962 \\
+\ 37 \\
\hline
9
\end{array}
$$

He was suddenly startled by a very loud *kachooga boop!* He dropped the chalk.

This was a bell nobody in the class had heard before, not even Mrs. Jewls.

Then came another *kachooga,* followed by two boops.

"What's it mean, Mrs. Jewls?" shouted Leslie.

"Everybody keep calm," said Mrs. Jewls.

*Kachooga boop! Boop! Boop!*

Mrs. Jewls hurried to the back closet.

It started up again.

*Kachooga boop!*

*Kachooga boop! Boop!*

Mrs. Jewls threw open the closet door and started tossing books and supplies out of the way.

*Kachooga boop! Boop! Boop!*

She finally removed a very large book, covered with dust.

*"The Complete Guide to Bells,"* said Terrence, reading the book's title over Mrs. Jewls's shoulder.

Mrs. Jewls sat on the floor, turning the pages until she got to the index. The kachooga booping continued, making it difficult for her to concentrate.

She found it. *"Kachooga boop–page 297."* She quickly turned to that page.

Suddenly, a loud *BOOM* shook the classroom. The lights went out.

This time nobody screamed. They were too scared.

Mrs. Jewls lit a candle. In the flickering light, she read aloud from page 297.

"If you hear a *kachooga*, followed by one, two, and then three boops, you should . . ." She stopped and blew a cloud of dust off the page, then tried to find where she had left off. ". . . one, two, and then three boops, you should run for your lives. A Cloud of Doom is about to destroy everything." She dropped the book. "Everybody outside!" she ordered.

Another *BOOM* shook the classroom so hard that the clock fell off the wall.

The children ran to the door, but it wouldn't open.

"The paper clip closet must have fallen over!" said Dameon. "It's blocking the door!"

"Paper clip closet?" asked Mrs. Jewls. She glared at Jason.

"Sorry," he said.

Jason couldn't keep a secret.

Todd, Maurecia, Dameon, and Allison all pushed together, but the door wouldn't budge.

"Let Stephen in there," urged Kathy. "He's been doing all those push-downs."

With Stephen's help, they pushed the door open.

Sirens wailed from the closet, which lay on the ground. A smoke screen filled the area.

In the light of Mrs. Jewls's candle, they could see that the chains and steel bar had been shattered. Paper clips were strewn all over the floor.

Benjamin and Rondi started picking them up.

"Leave them!" shouted Mrs. Jewls.

Now they knew it was serious.

Mrs. Jewls told everyone to hold hands as she led the way down the staircase.

Paul grabbed Leslie's pigtail.

"What are you doing?" she demanded.

"It's either that or your hand," he said.

"Okay, then," Leslie agreed.

The kachooga booping continued as more loud booms shook the school.

A gust of wind blew out Mrs. Jewls's candle, and the class continued down in darkness.

Joe stepped on a skateboard, which somebody had left in the middle of the stairs. He fell, pulling John down with him. Who pulled down Dana. Who pulled down Jenny. Who pulled down Rondi. Who pulled down Terrence. The chain reaction ended with Dameon pulling down Mrs. Jewls.

The class lay sprawled across the stairs as the school shook around them.

"We're doomed!" Mac wailed.

"Look!" exclaimed Bebe.

A door had opened, and there was a light coming from inside a classroom.

A teacher stood in the doorway. "Quick. Come inside," she beckoned. "You'll be safe here."

She had a long fingernail on her pinky.

# 28

# THE TEACHER WITH
# THE LONG FINGERNAIL

Like moths, the children went to the light.

"Welcome, welcome, glad you're here, come in," the woman said as they filed past and joined the other kids in her class

"I'm sorry I don't have enough desks, but we'll make do. Please find a place on the floor for now."

The children did as they were told. They felt safe, even if a bit uncomfortable. They could no longer feel the school shake, or hear the kachooga boops.

"Miss Zarves," said Mrs. Jewls. "It's so good to see you! How long has it been?"

"Feels like forever," said Miss Zarves.

"I never bump into you in the teachers' lounge," said Mrs. Jewls. "We must just keep missing each other."

"I try not to bump into people," said Miss Zarves.

Miss Zarves was tall and thin. Her skirt and blouse were neat and trim. Her short hair looked shiny and silky, and smelled like strawberry shampoo. Everything about her was neat and orderly, except for that one fingernail.

"And how's Mavis?" asked Miss Zarves.

Mavis was Mrs. Jewls's daughter.

"Adorable," said Mrs. Jewls. "But they grow up so fast, don't they?"

"I wouldn't know," said Miss Zarves.

"You don't look like you've aged a day," said Mrs. Jewls.

"Very nice of you to say," said Miss Zarves.

Mrs. Jewls wasn't just being nice. Miss Zarves hadn't changed one bit—except for her fingernail, of course, which had grown considerably longer.

Calvin walked between the two teachers. "Excuse me, Miss Zarves," he said. "I think I'm supposed to give you this."

He handed Miss Zarves a folded piece of paper that was so old, it tore as Miss Zarves unfolded it. She strained to read the faded writing.

"Oh, okay," she said to Mrs. Jewls, then dropped the note in the trash.

"Is that the note I gave you to give Miss Zarves?" Mrs. Jewls asked Calvin.

Calvin shrugged. "I just found it in my pocket," he said, sounding even more surprised than Mrs. Jewls.

Mrs. Jewls stared at him. "You told me you gave it to her," she accused.

"I don't think I ever said that," said Calvin.

Mrs. Jewls continued to stare as he returned to his seat on the floor.

"We were just about to have our history

review," said Miss Zarves. "Who's your best history student?"

"Myron," Mrs. Jewls answered, without hesitation.

Myron had gotten the highest score on the history portion of the Ultimate Test.

"Myron, stand up, please," said Miss Zarves. He stood.

"What kind of shoes did Mary Bopkins like to wear?" Miss Zarves asked him.

"Who?" asked Myron.

The kids from Miss Zarves's class giggled.

"No laughing," said Miss Zarves. "We don't laugh at stupid people. Don't feel bad, Myron. You may be stupid now, but once you've been in my class for a few years, you'll know the history of everybody. Mark, would you please tell Myron the answer."

*A few years?*" Myron asked, but Miss Zarves ignored the question.

Mark Miller stood up. "Which Mary Bopkins do you mean?" he asked. "The one born in 1801 in Boston, or the one born in 1954 in San Francisco?"

"Boston," said Miss Zarves.

"Red boots," said Mark.

"Excellent," said Miss Zarves.

"Who's Mary Bopkins?" asked Mrs. Jewls. "Was she famous?"

"Why?" asked Miss Zarves. "Does your class only study famous people? Do you think famous people are more important than people who aren't famous?"

"But there isn't enough time to study *every-one*," said Mrs. Jewls.

"We don't play favorites in my class," said Miss Zarves.

She went to the back closet and took out several giant stacks of papers. "This is everyone born in 1837." She went around the room, handing each student a stack of a hundred pages or more. "When you finish studying a page, please pass it on to someone else."

Myron stared helplessly at his stack. "I can't even read this," he complained. "I think it's Chinese."

"Well, yes, a lot of people were born in China," said Miss Zarves.

She handed Myron a Chinese dictionary and said, "You'll need this."

It is impossible to say how long Myron sat there, fumbling through the dictionary as the kids around him were passing around their sheets of paper.

He might have been there an hour. Or a day. Or a week.

Time passes slowly when you're trying to read a Chinese dictionary.

Even if you're Chinese.

He glanced up and spotted a pair of scissors on Mark Miller's desk. He got an idea.

"Hey, Mark, can I borrow those for a sec?" Myron asked.

"Sure," said Mark.

Myron took the scissors, then walked bravely to the front of the room.

He didn't know if his plan would work. In fact, it really didn't make any sense, but it was his only h-o-p-e.

"Excuse me, Miss Zarves. I can trim your

fingernail for you, if you like," he offered.

"My fingernail?" asked Miss Zarves, astonished by such a suggestion. "Which one?"

"The long one on the end," said Myron.

Miss Zarves looked at her hand. "Hmm, now that you mention it, it has gotten long. I guess I hadn't noticed, because it grew so slowly."

She held out her hand.

Myron pressed hard on the scissors and snipped it off.

"That does feel better," said Miss Zarves. "Thank you, Myron."

Myron held the fingernail up in the air.

Except, he was no longer standing in the front of the classroom. He was standing on the stairs, and everyone else from Mrs. Jewls's class lay sprawled across the staircase.

"A million!" he shouted triumphantly.

# 29

## AFTER THE STORM

The boops and booms had stopped, and the lights were back on.

Myron and the others had to step over all sorts of objects as they made their way back up toward their classroom. The stairs were strewn with books, papers, cafeteria trays, musical instruments, an air pump, a giant stuffed walrus, and even a bust of Sigmund Freud.

Between the twenty-sixth and twenty-seventh floors, the stairs were completely blocked off by Mr. Kidswatter's enormous desk. They all had fun climbing over it, including Mrs. Jewls.

Once back in class, Myron dropped Miss Zarves's fingernail into the bucket, which, unfortunately, was empty. Sadly, the other nine hundred thousand, nine hundred, and ninety-nine clippings were gone.

Myron would have written 1,000,000 on the blackboard anyway, but there was no blackboard.

The chalk was there, however.

It was as if everything inside Wayside School had been shuffled like a deck of cards and dealt out randomly to every floor.

(Mrs. Jewls's blackboard was eventually discovered in the library. Fingernails and toenails would continue to be found for years to come, sometimes in very strange places.)

The sun shined. The sky was as blue as Allison's eyes. Birds chirped as they flew about.

There had been no birds during the dark days of doom.

Louis, the yard teacher, shoveled snow off the roof. Among other things, the cloud had dumped huge amounts of snow. The playground sparkled white.

Louis had to be careful. The snow was packed high above the guardrails and was very slippery. "Look out, below!" he shouted as he tossed a shovelful of snow over the edge.

Down below the kids were playing a kind of reverse dodgeball. It was the boys against the girls. Every time Louis shouted, "Look out below!" they did the opposite.

Eric Ovens charged past Jenny and dived face-first, sliding across the snow-covered ground. Louis's clump smacked him right on the head.

"One point!" he exclaimed.

Recess was three hours today. The kids had been sent out to play, while the teachers were stuck with cleaning up the mess made by the storm.

Just as Mrs. Jewls had predicted, now that the

Cloud of Doom was gone, the world had become a happier place. The only thing missing was a rainbow.

"Look out below!" Louis called from the other side of the school.

They raced around the building. Leslie dived toward the falling clump. "One point," she declared.

"No way, Miss Piggy-tails," said Terrence. "It missed you!"

"Did not!" Leslie insisted. "See, look at all the snow in my hair."

"That's ground snow," argued Terrence.

Dana came to Leslie's defense. "Some of it came from the ground," she agreed. "But four flakes came from the air. I saw them."

"How can you see four snowflakes?" asked Paul.

"Super glasses!" said Dana, pointing to her spectacles. She picked four snowflakes out of Leslie's hair. "One, two, three, and four. Just like I told you."

"That proves it!" declared Bebe. "One point!"

Paul scowled. He remained skeptical of her spectacles.

Up on the roof, Louis spotted something sticking out of the snow. It was purple and green, with some yellow dots.

He tried to pull it free, but it was stuck. He pulled hard.

It still wouldn't budge.

He gave it one hard yank!

The umbrella jerked free, but Louis's feet slipped out from under him. He fell on his bottom and slid backward across the roof.

"Look out below!" he shouted as he went over the edge.

The children ran to the call. They were quite surprised when they looked up and saw the yard teacher coming toward them.

Louis looked down. He didn't want to hurt the children.

He considered trying a Mary Poppins, but he was holding the wrong end of the umbrella, and there wasn't time to change his grip and try to open it.

His best chance was to grab the top of the flagpole.

Wayside School had an extra-tall flagpole so it wouldn't look puny next to the building.

Louis reached out for it but missed.

The next thing he knew, he was spinning wildly in circles.

The curved handle of the umbrella had hooked the pole.

Louis whirled dizzily around it as he slowly moved down the pole. By the time he reached the ground, he must have circled the flagpole more than a thousand times.

Sharie ran to him.

To Louis, it looked like there were six Sharies, all spinning like tops.

"Thanks, Louis—you're the best!" said Sharie, taking her umbrella. "But really, there was no big rush. You could have just used the stairs."

# 30

# RAINBOW

There was no stove in the cafeteria kitchen. An enormous pot hung from a thick chain above a blazing fire.

"Lower the pot," ordered Miss Mush.

Mr. Pepperadder turned the squeaky crank, and the pot came down.

"What will it be today?" he asked.

"Shh!" said Miss Mush.

Mr. Pepperadder knew better. You must never interrupt a great artist during her moment of inspiration.

Miss Mush's eyes were closed. She rubbed her chin. She wanted to make something truly special after the Storm of Doom. "Rainbow stew!" she declared as she raised her wooden spoon high above her head.

"Brilliant!" agreed Mr. Pepperadder.

"What do we have that's red?" asked Miss Mush.

Mr. Pepperadder looked over his inventory list. "Red cabbage," he said. "Beets, strawberries, red peppers."

Miss Mush waved the wooden spoon and said, "Toss them in the pot!"

Flames shot up as Mr. Pepperadder threw in the ingredients. He had to shield his eyes from the smoke.

"What about yellow?" asked Miss Mush.

"Yellow squash, bananas, yellow peppers, yellow onions . . ."

"Start with the bananas," said Miss Mush,

"and then we'll see about the onions."

Mr. Pepperadder started to peel a banana, but Miss Mush stopped him.

"The peel is the part that's yellow," she reminded him. "If I wanted white, I would have asked for peeled bananas."

"Sorry," said Mr. Pepperadder. He tossed fifty-seven bushels of bananas, peels and all, into the pot.

There was a loud hissing noise, as steam filled the room.

Some cooks considered things like taste, or perhaps nutrition, when preparing a meal. For rainbow stew, color was all that mattered.

Miss Mush stirred the pot with a large stick. "Perhaps a little black now, for definition," she said.

Mr. Pepperadder read from his list. "Poppy seeds, burnt toast, my shoes . . ."

High above them, in Mrs. Jewls's class, several children held their noses.

"What's that smell?" asked Calvin.

"Miss Mush must be cooking something," said Bebe.

"It smells like shoes," said Myron.

D.J. sniffed. "Black shoes," he said. "With hard soles, and no laces."

"You can smell the laces?" asked Kathy.

"No," said D.J. "I just told you there weren't any laces."

Mr. Kidswatter's voice came over the speaker. "GOOD MORNING, STUDENTS. IT'S ANOTHER GREAT DAY HERE AT—"

There was the sound of paper rustling.

"—WAYSIDE SCHOOL. FOR LUNCH TODAY, MISS MUSH WILL BE SERVING RAINBOW STEW. IT WILL BE THE GREATEST LUNCH EVER!"

Fifteen floors beneath them, Miss Mush felt her stomach tighten. She too heard Mr. Kidswatter's morning announcement. Now the pressure was on.

She climbed a ladder and stared down into the bubbling pot. Her face was covered with soot and sweat. "Something orange," she decided.

"How about oranges?" suggested Mr. Pepperadder.

"Too obvious," said Miss Mush.

"Carrots?"

"I suppose . . ." said Miss Mush, although carrots didn't *feel* right to her.

Inspiration struck! "Eighteen pumpkins!" she exclaimed.

Each pumpkin made a giant splash, as Miss Mush and Mr. Pepperadder took turns tossing them into the pot.

After all the pumpkins were added to the stew, a tiny smile crept across Miss Mush's face.

It was a smile that all great artists know well. After years of self-doubt, she started to believe that she was on the verge of creating something truly wonderful.

But it was just a quick smile, and then back to work!

The doubts always return.

The lunch bell kaboinked, and the children descended upon the cafeteria.

"Rainbow Stew," said Benjamin. "It sounds like it could be good."

"Don't let the name fool you," warned Todd. "The better the name, the worse it tastes."

"Remember when she made 'Midnight Madness'?" asked Paul.

"Don't even say it!" snapped Leslie. "I was up all night, running around in circles."

Miss Mush and Mr. Pepperadder stood shoulder to shoulder as the children lined up. They had finished the stew only moments before.

"I hope they like it," Miss Mush whispered.

"They will," Mr. Pepperadder assured her. He wore short pants, black socks, and no shoes.

Miss Mush hoped he was right, but all her doubts had returned. Her apron was splotched with lots of bright colors, but the rainbow stew looked like lumpy grayish-brown mud.

She didn't understand it. What had happened to all the colors?

Maurecia reached the front of the line. Miss Mush scooped some rainbow stew into a bowl and handed it to her.

"Thank you, Miss Mush," said Maurecia, always polite.

"Sorry, it was supposed to be a bit more colorful," explained Miss Mush. "I don't know what went wrong."

Joy was next.

"Sorry," Miss Mush said again as she handed a bowl to Joy.

"Sorry, Ron," she said. "Sorry, Deedee. Sorry, Joe. Sorry, John. Sorry, sorry, sorry . . . ."

Allison and Rondi sat at one end of a long table. "Are you going to eat it?" Rondi asked Allison.

"I have a tangerine in my pocket," said Allison. "Maybe I'll just eat that."

Rondi watched as Allison slowly removed the entire peel in just one piece.

Deedee counted the points on her fork.

D.J. swirled his plastic fork through the gray muck. "Well, here goes," he announced.

He poked his fork into something solid. It could have been a vegetable, or maybe a piece of meat, or perhaps part of a shoe.

He lowered his fork. "Maybe later," he said.

"Looks delicious!" Kathy said enthusiastically. She took a big spoonful, brought it to her mouth, and swallowed.

"Yummy!" she declared.

The other kids couldn't be sure. They could never tell anymore when Kathy was speaking in opposites.

Calvin stabbed something gooey with his fork. He brought it to his mouth, chewed a while, and then chewed some more.

"Well?" asked Bebe.

Calvin wasn't sure how to describe it. "Red," he said at last.

"Red?" questioned Allison. "That's a color, not a taste."

"And blue," said Calvin.

Rondi took a bite. She chewed awhile. "Purple!" she declared.

"I taste yellow!" said Todd.

Dana swallowed. "Pink!" she exclaimed.

John finished chewing, then swallowed. "Kind

of a blue green," he said.

"It's delicious," said Sharie. "Purple and green with yellow polka dots."

The more they chewed, the more colors they tasted.

"That's silly," said Allison. She took a bite.

Her eyes shone. She tasted orange, with green and purple stripes, and a black outline.

"Do you like it?" asked Rondi.

"Only the best lunch ever!" said Allison.


Mr. Pepperadder grabbed and shook Miss Mush's arm. "They like it!" he said excitedly. "Look at them! They really like it."

Miss Mush didn't say a word. A tear rolled down her sweaty and sooty cheek.

"Did you write down the recipe?" he asked.

Miss Mush shook her head. "There is no recipe," she whispered. "No two rainbows are the same."

She gazed out across the lunchroom. This was all she ever wanted.

Everybody chewed.